MORE PRAISE FOR BABYMOUSE!

"Sassy, smart . . . Babymouse is here to stay."
—**The Horn Book Magazine**

"Young readers will happily fall in line."
—**Kirkus Reviews**

"The brother-sister creative team hits the mark with humor, sweetness, and characters so genuine they can pass for real kids." —**Booklist**

"Babymouse is spunky, ambitious, and, at times, a total dweeb."
—**School Library Journal**

Be sure to read **all** the **BABYMOUSE** books:

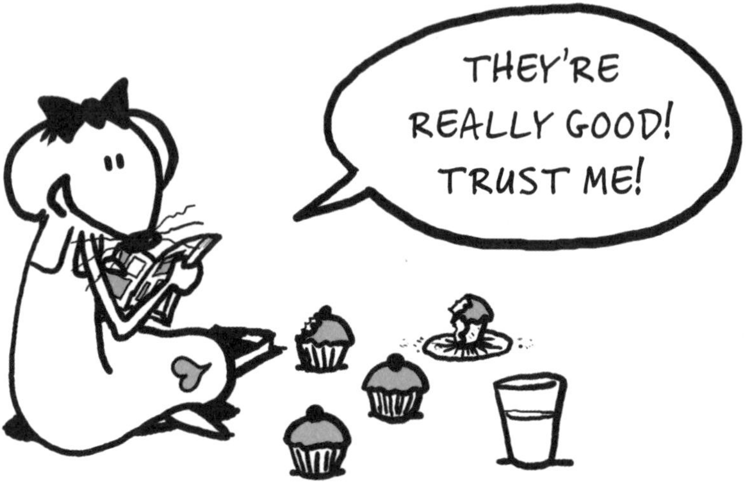
THEY'RE REALLY GOOD! TRUST ME!

BABYMOUSE
OUR HERO

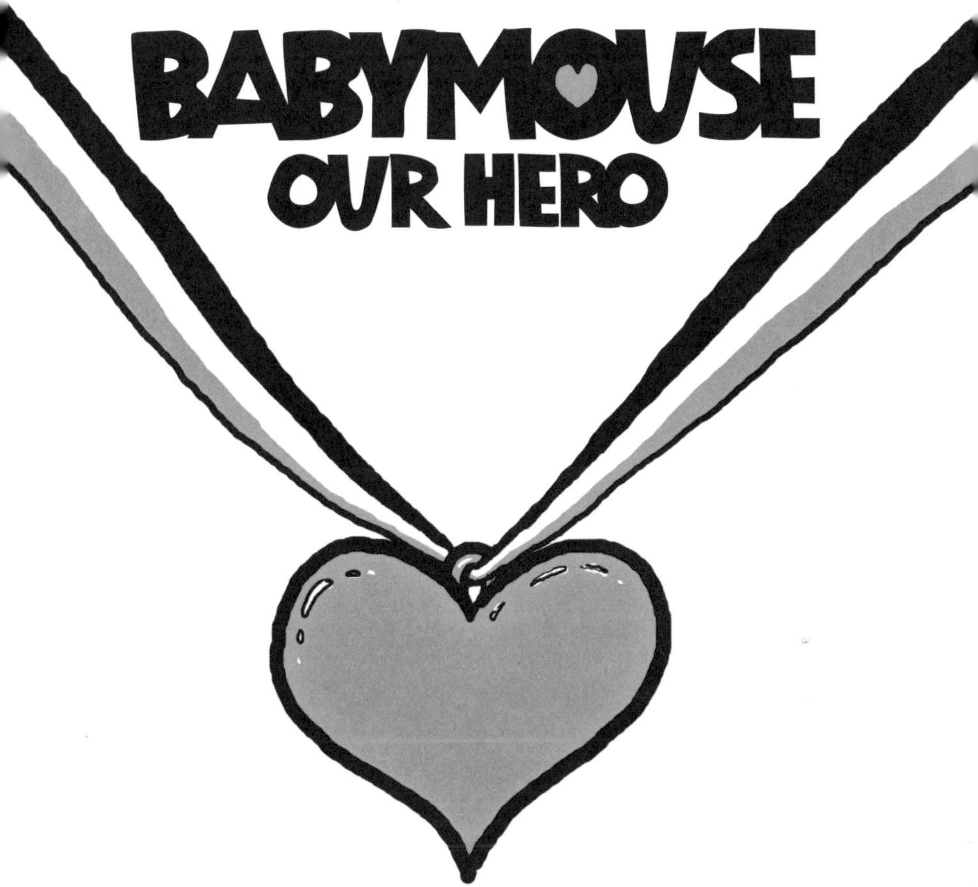

BY JENNIFER L. HOLM & MATTHEW HOLM

RANDOM HOUSE NEW YORK

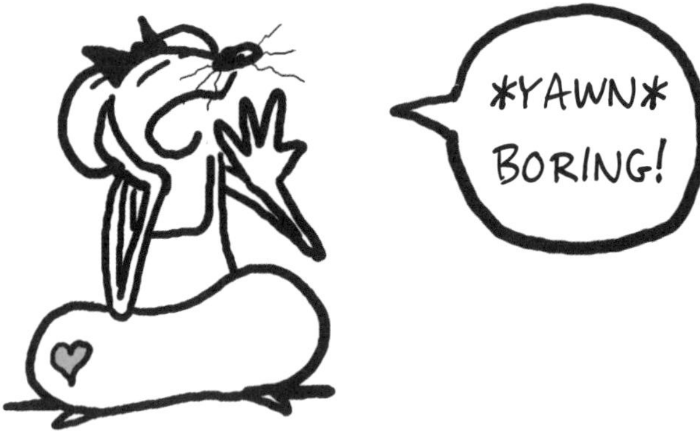
YAWN
BORING!

 Published in the United States by Random House Children's Books, a division of Random House, Inc., New York, and simultaneously in Canada by Random House of Canada Limited, Toronto.

www.randomhouse.com/kids
www.babymouse.com

Library of Congress Cataloging-in-Publication Data
Holm, Jennifer L.
Babymouse : our hero / Jennifer Holm and Matthew Holm
p. cm.
SUMMARY: An imaginative young mouse is terrified to face her enemy in dodgeball, but with the help of her best friend, she not only plays the game, she proves herself a hero.
ISBN 978-0-375-83230-7 (trade) — ISBN 978-0-375-93230-4 (lib. bdg.)
[1. Ball games—Fiction. 2. Fear—Fiction. 3. Schools—Fiction. 4. Heroes—Fiction. 5. Mice—Fiction. 6. Animals—Fiction. 7. Cartoons and comics.]
I. Holm, Matthew. II. Title.
PN6727.H592 B32 2005 741.5'973—dc22 2004051169

MANUFACTURED IN MALAYSIA 16 15 14 13 12 11 10 9 8

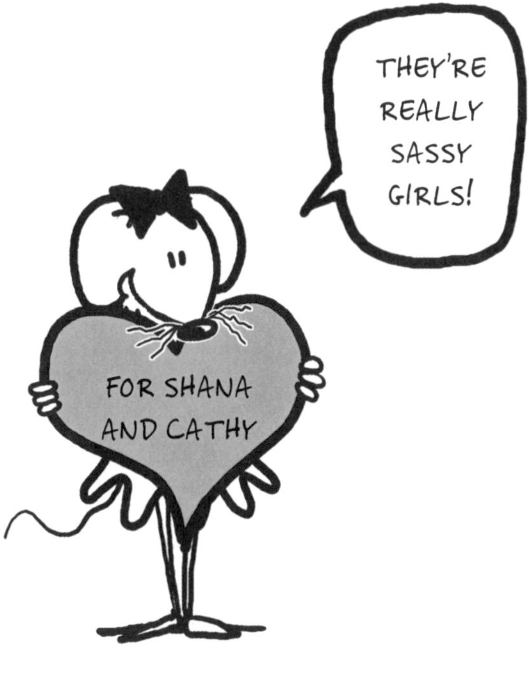
THEY'RE REALLY SASSY GIRLS!
FOR SHANA AND CATHY

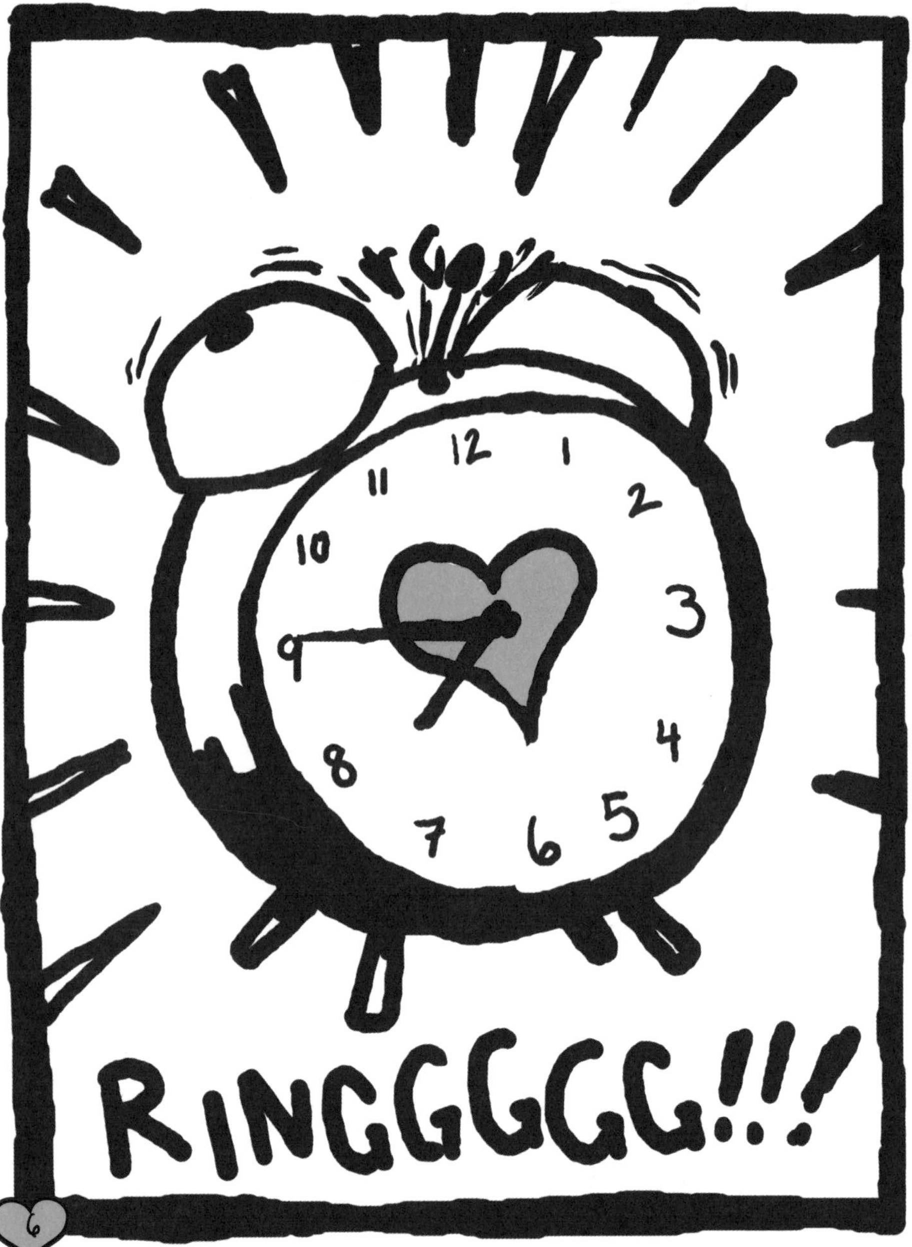
RINGGGGG!!!

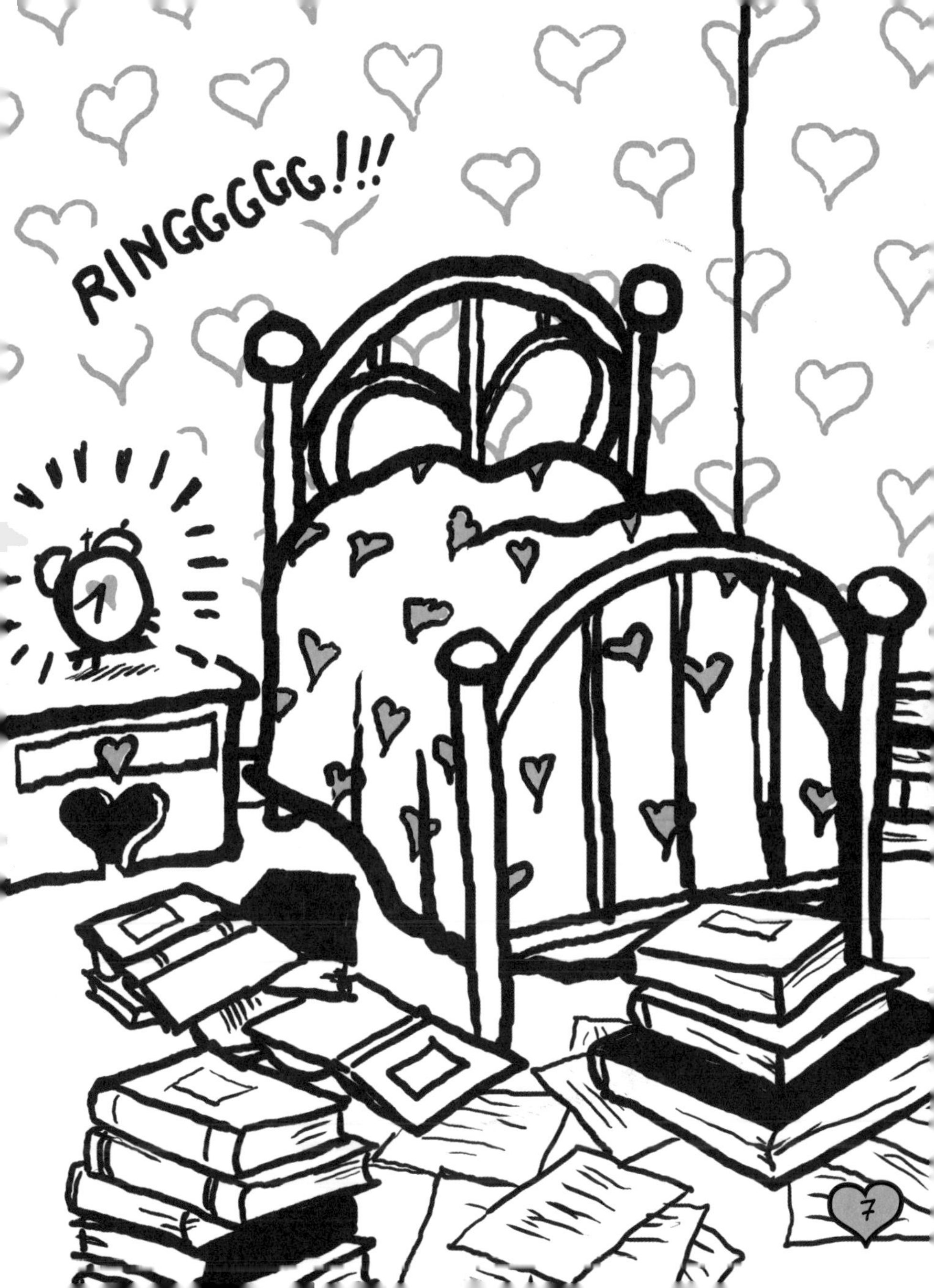
RINGGGGG!!!

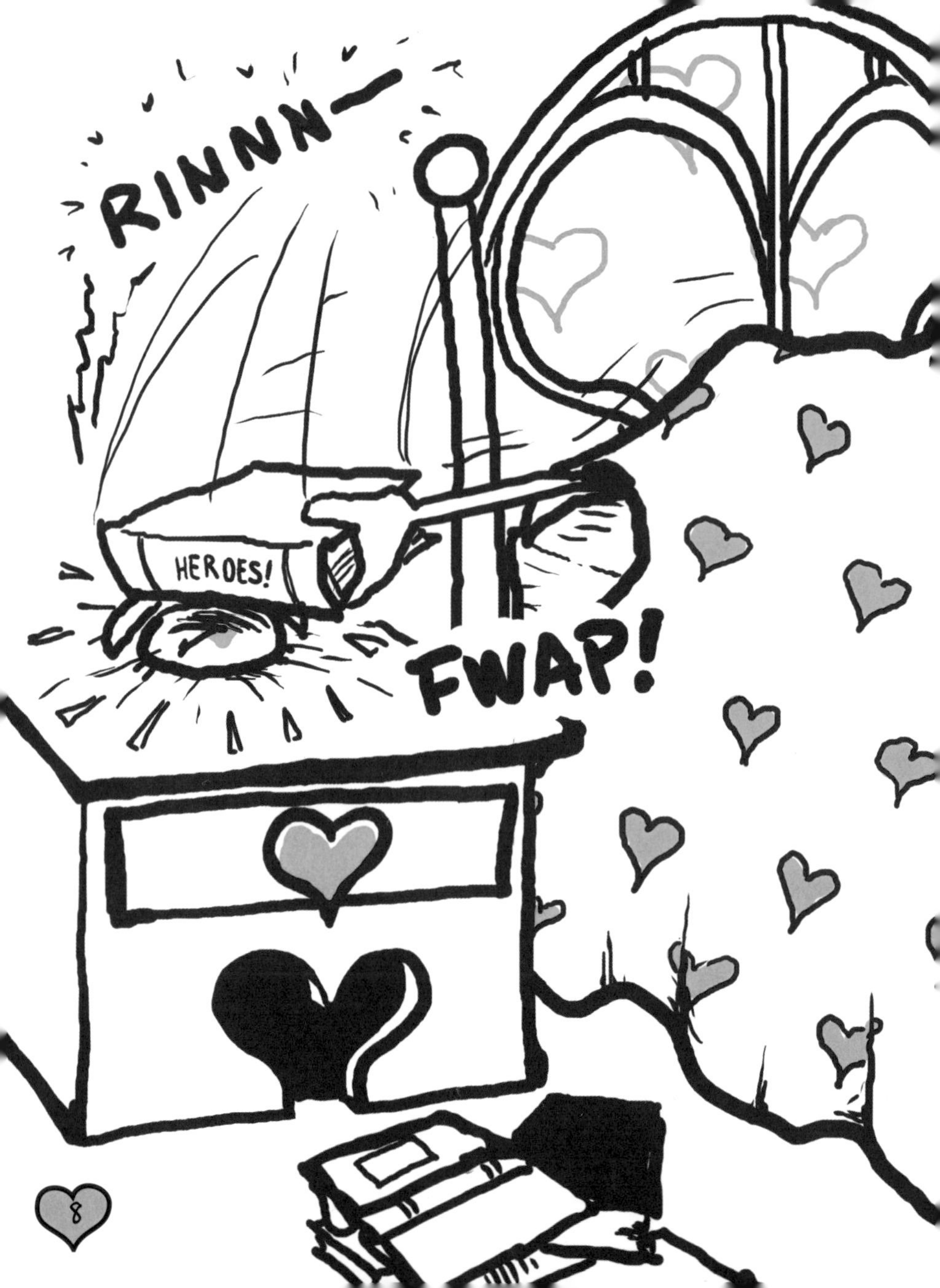
RINNN—
HEROES!
FWAP!

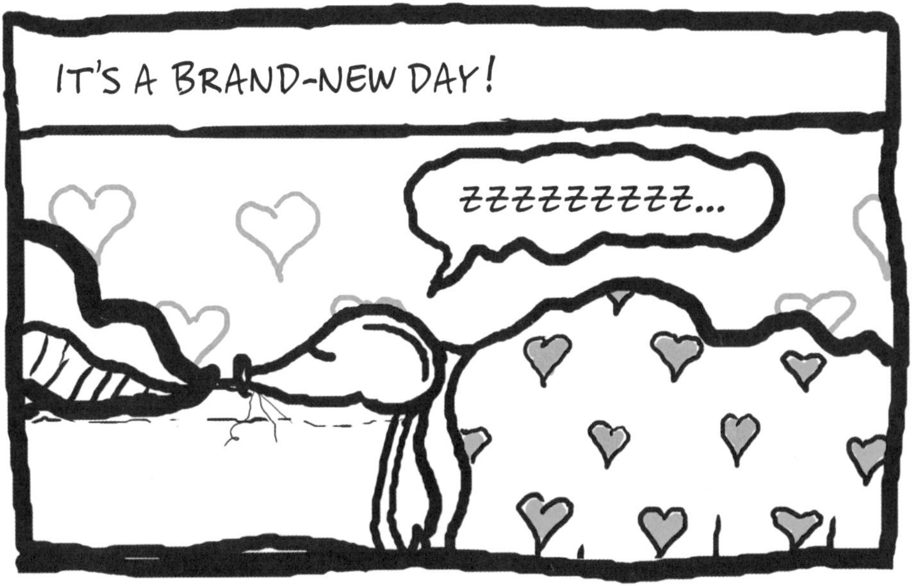
IT'S A BRAND-NEW DAY!
ZZZZZZZZZZ...

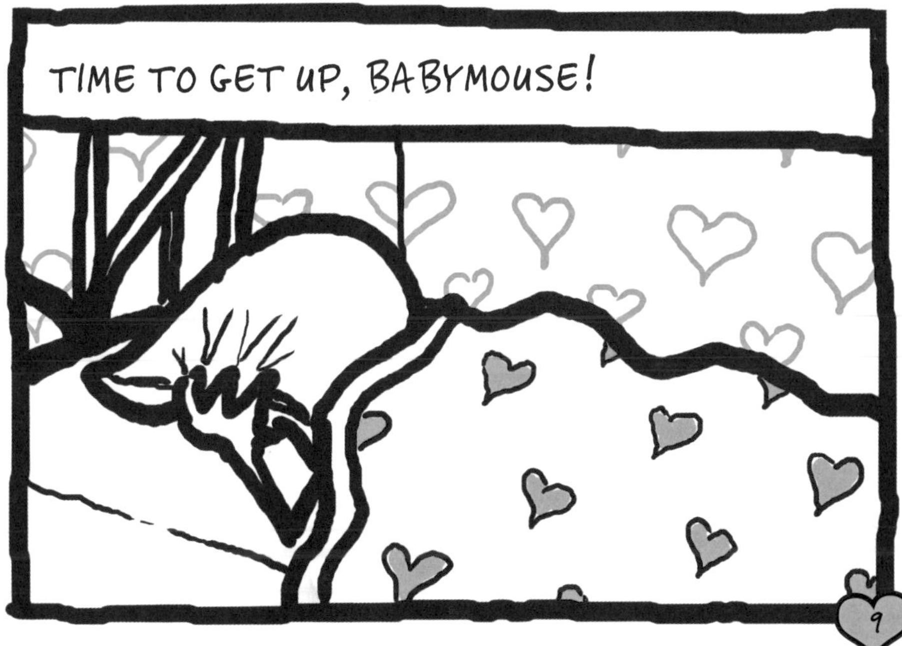
TIME TO GET UP, BABYMOUSE!

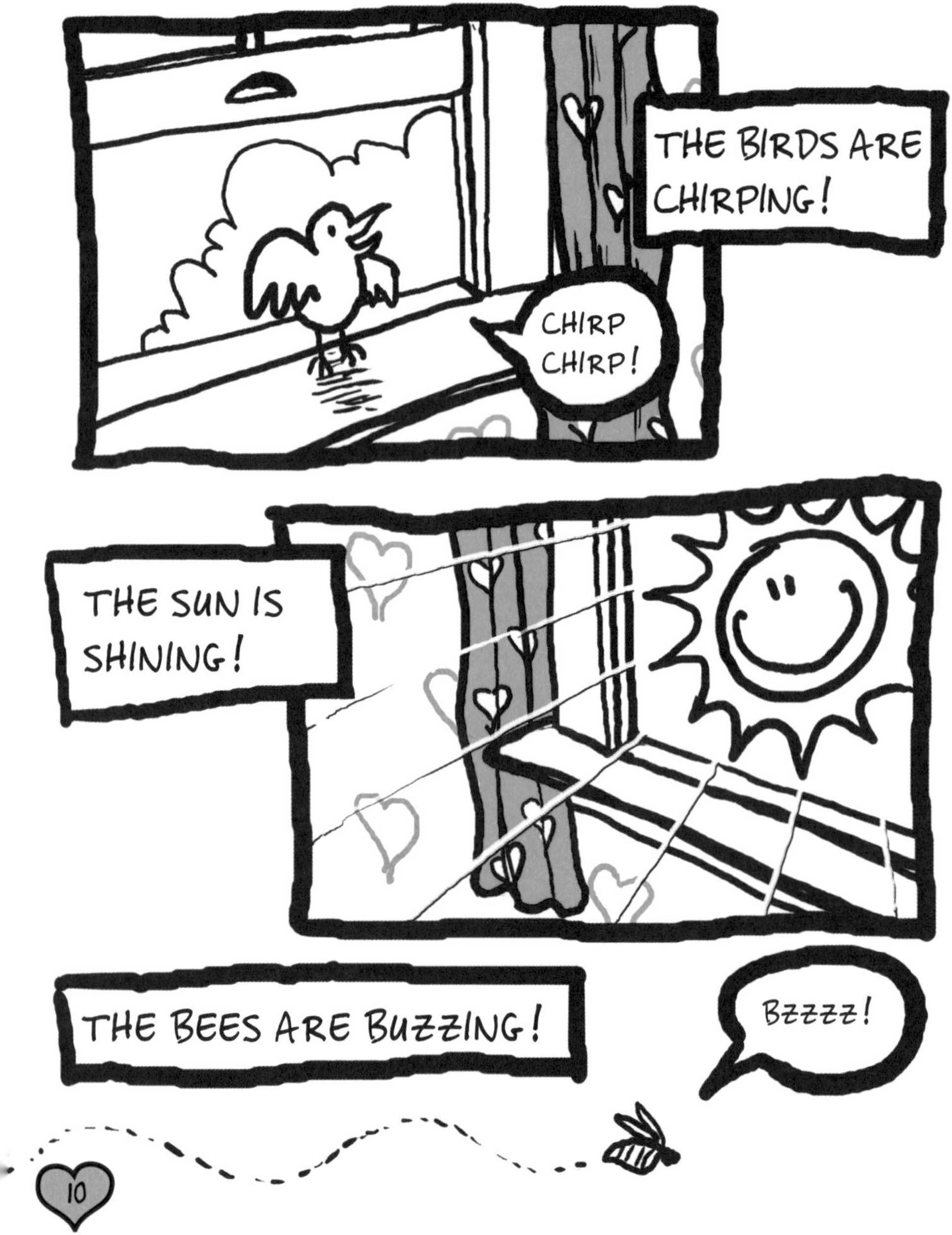
THE BIRDS ARE CHIRPING!
CHIRP CHIRP!
THE SUN IS SHINING!
THE BEES ARE BUZZING!
Bzzzz!

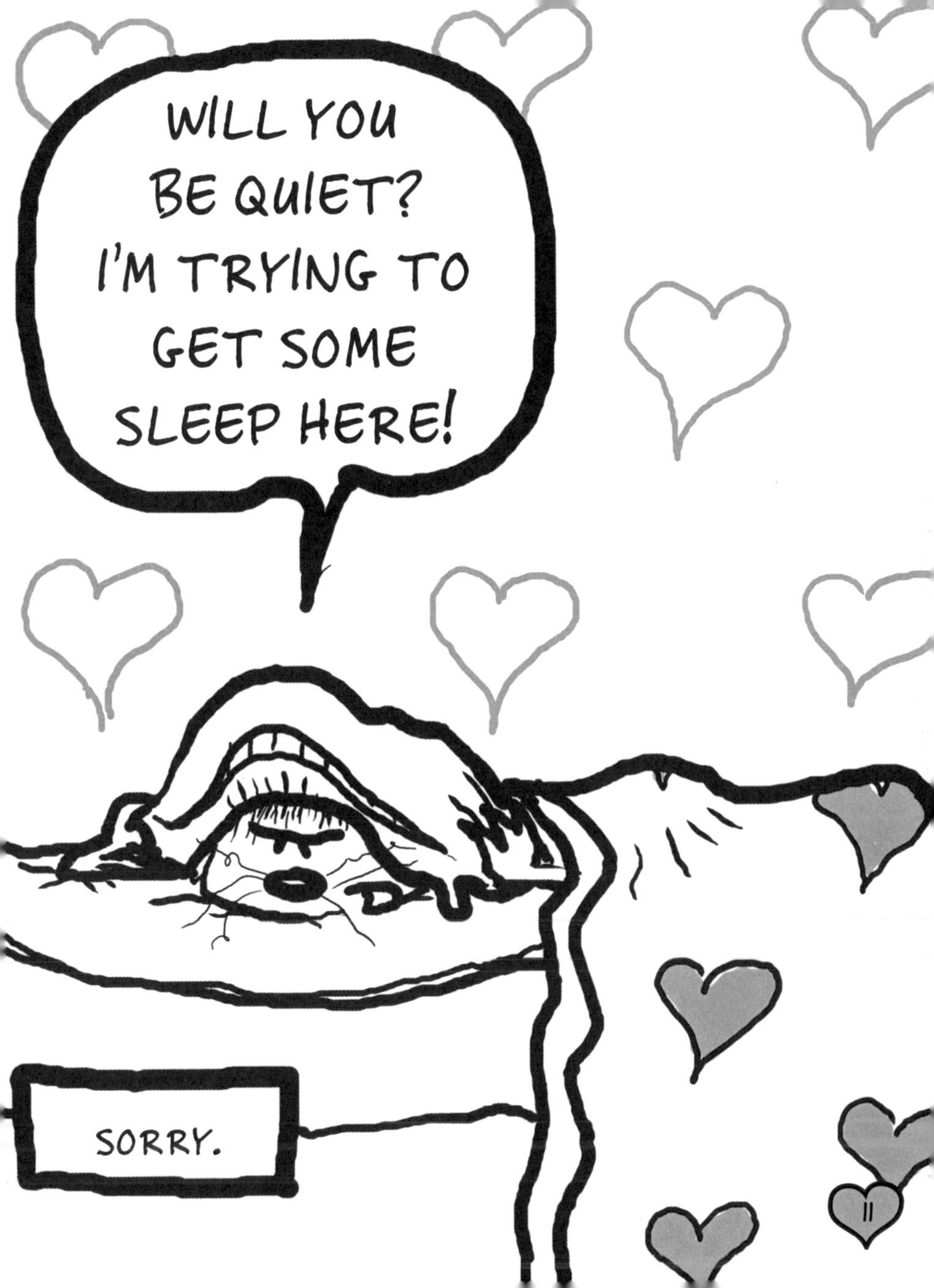
WILL YOU BE QUIET? I'M TRYING TO GET SOME SLEEP HERE!
SORRY.
11

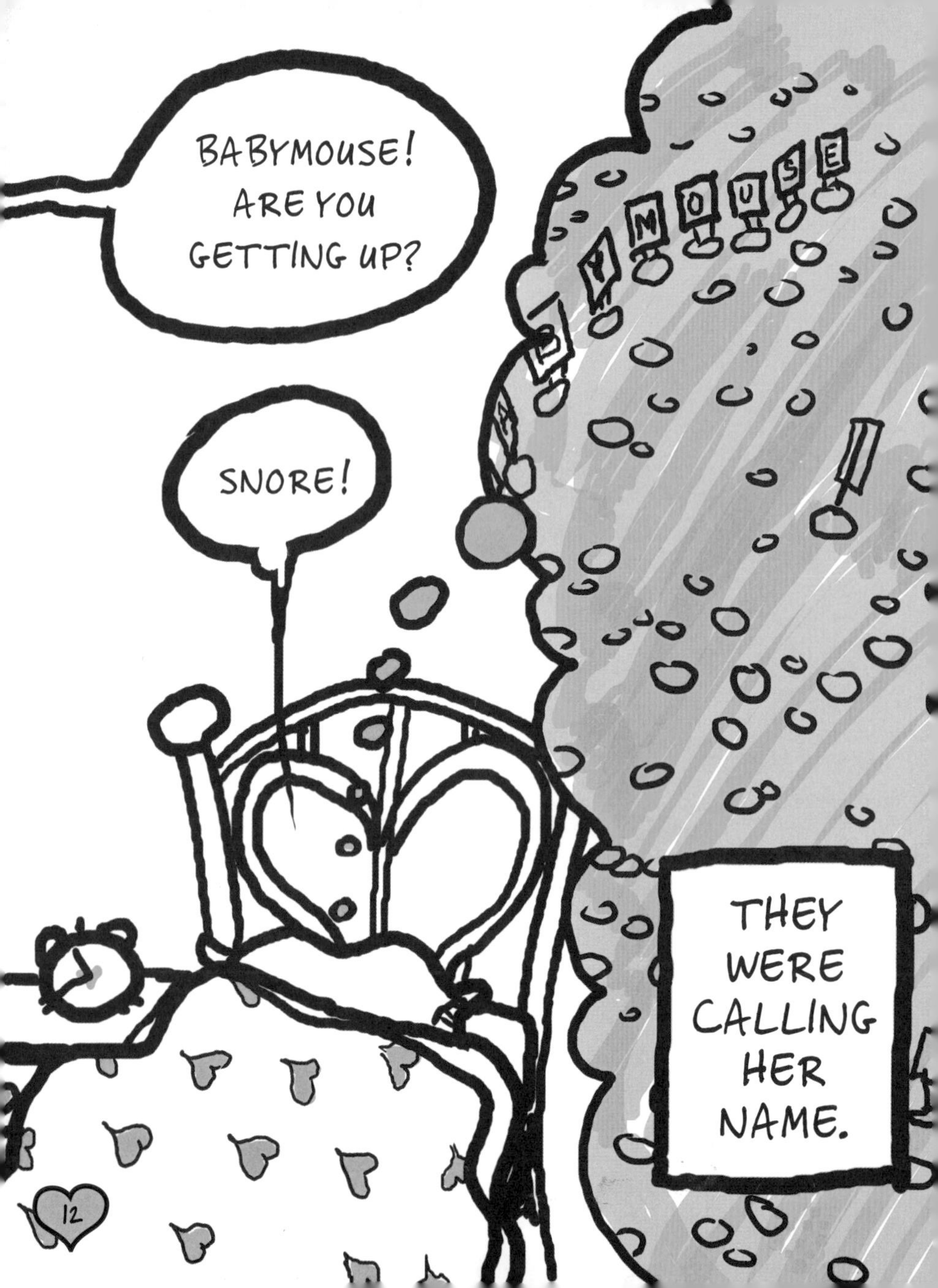
BABYMOUSE! ARE YOU GETTING UP?
SNORE!
THEY WERE CALLING HER NAME.

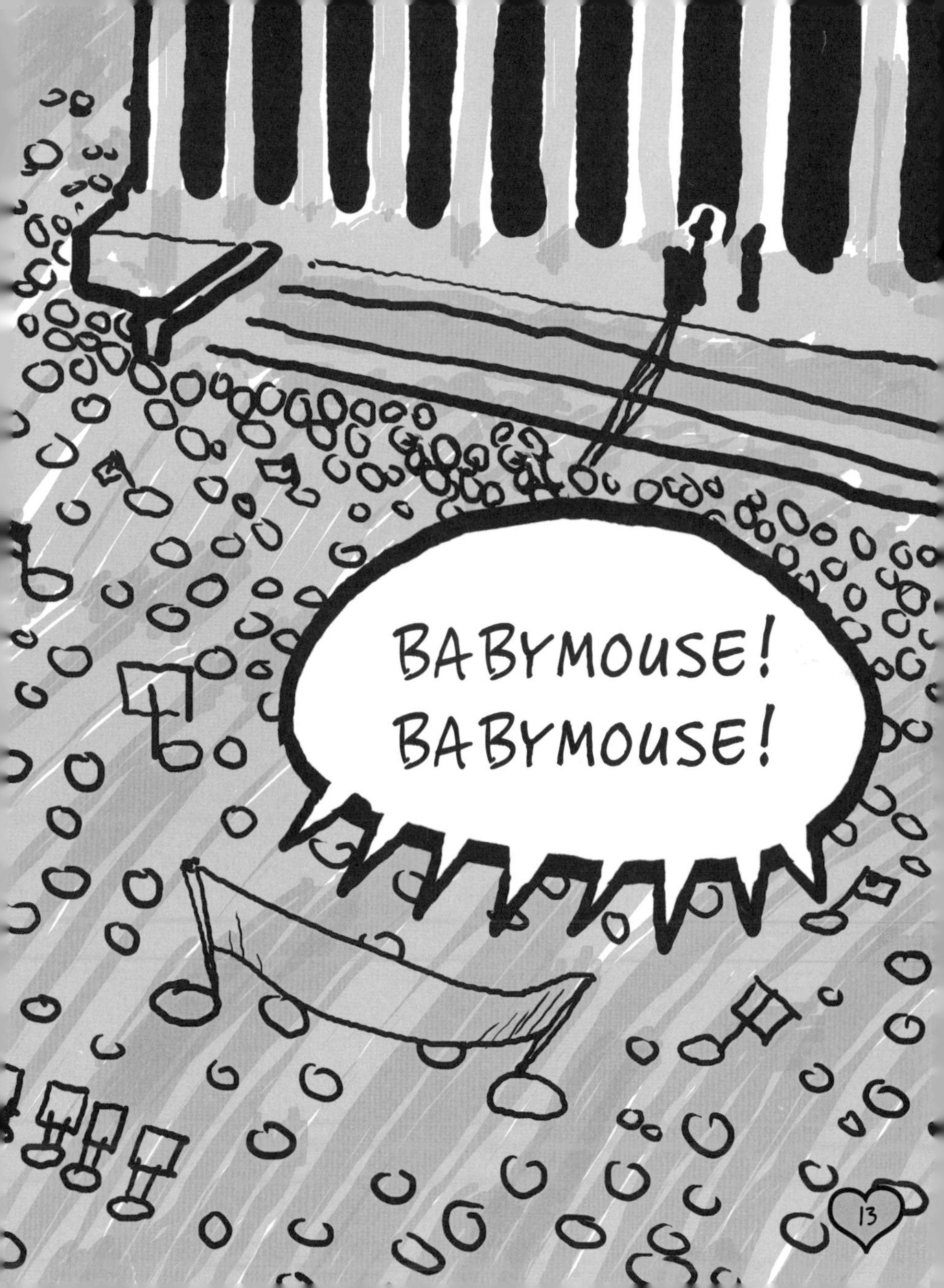
BABYMOUSE! BABYMOUSE!

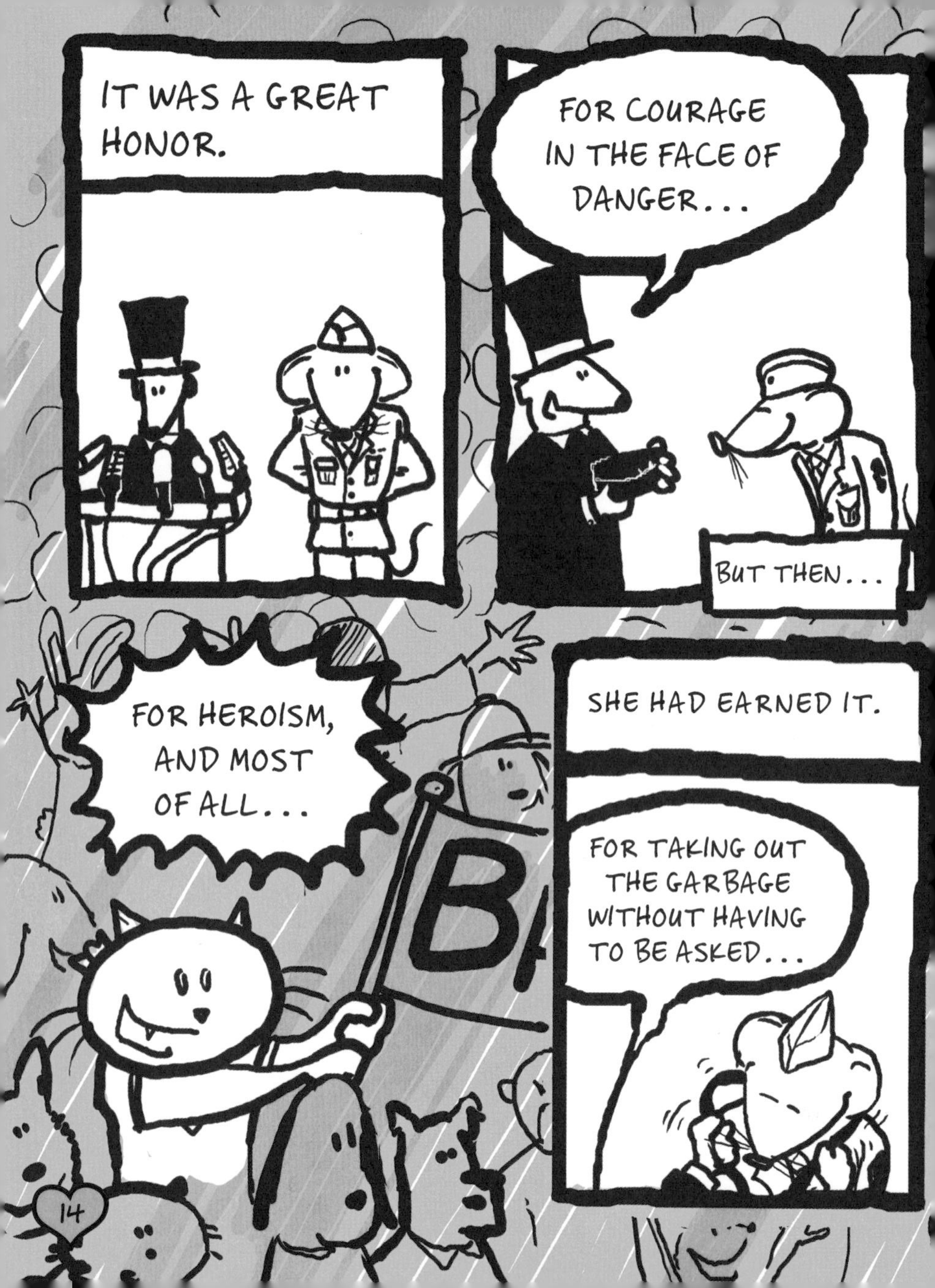
IT WAS A GREAT HONOR.
FOR COURAGE IN THE FACE OF DANGER...
BUT THEN...
FOR HEROISM, AND MOST OF ALL...
SHE HAD EARNED IT.
FOR TAKING OUT THE GARBAGE WITHOUT HAVING TO BE ASKED...

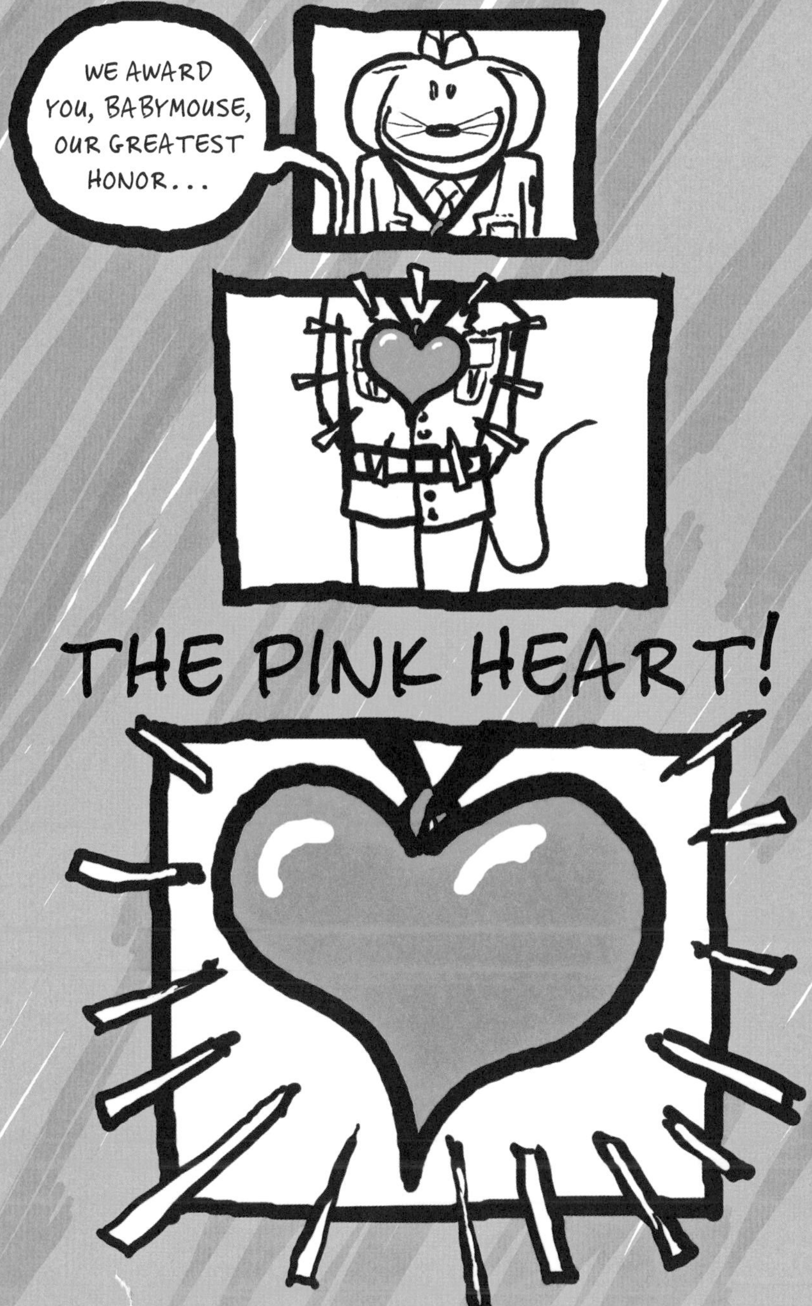

WE AWARD YOU, BABYMOUSE, OUR GREATEST HONOR...
THE PINK HEART!

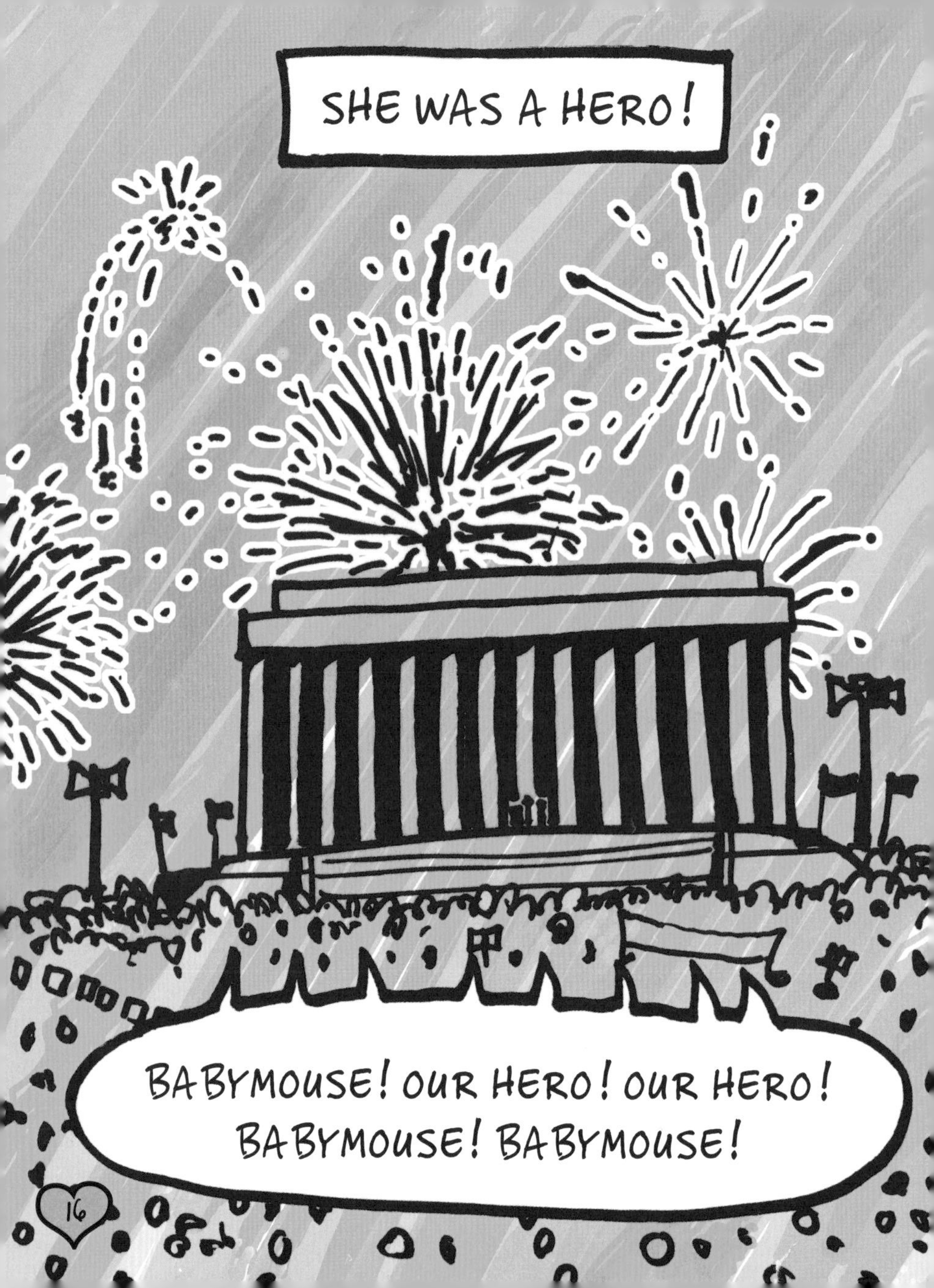
SHE WAS A HERO!
BABYMOUSE! OUR HERO! OUR HERO! BABYMOUSE! BABYMOUSE!

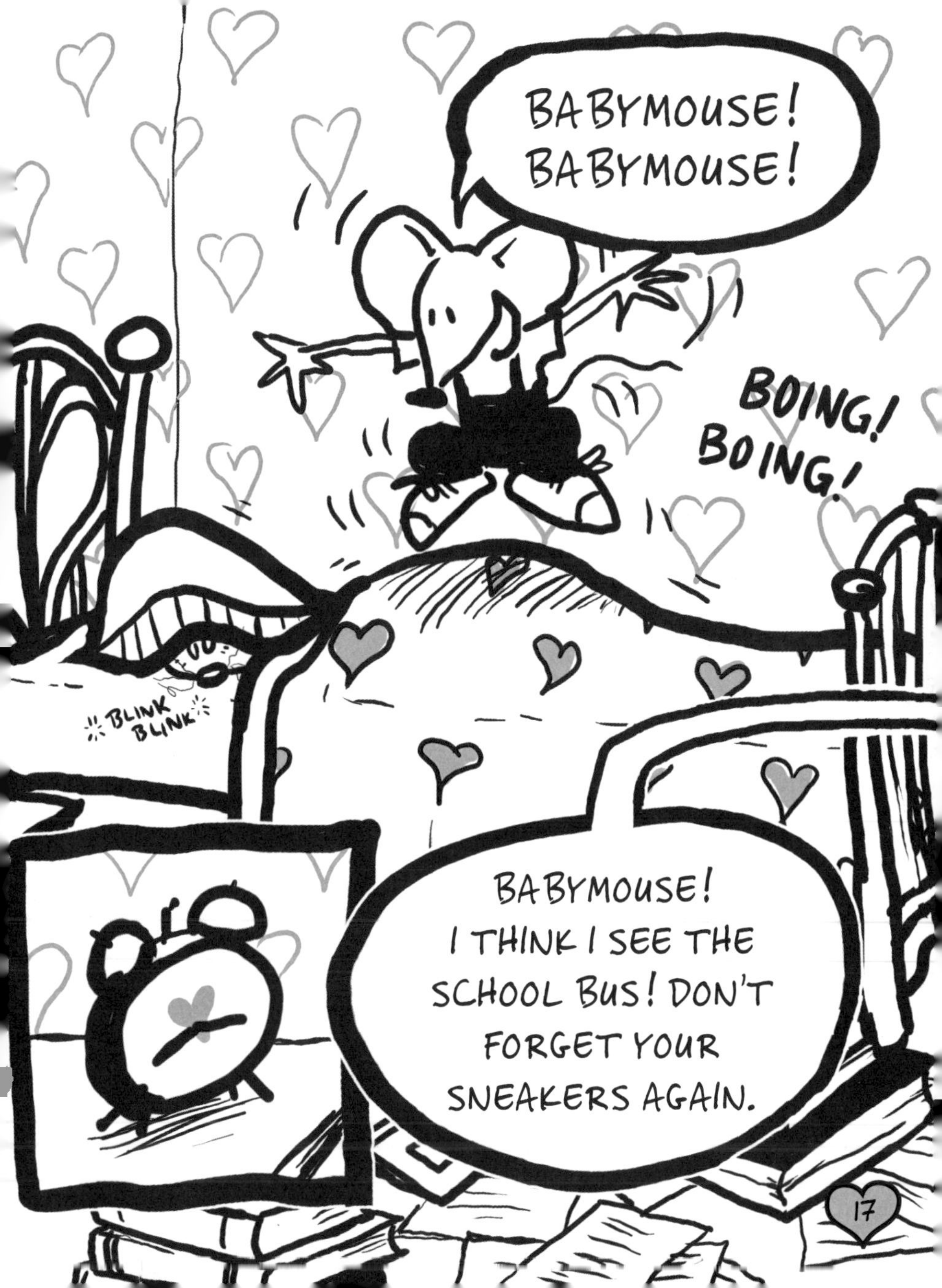
BABYMOUSE! BABYMOUSE!
BOING! BOING!
BLINK BLINK
BABYMOUSE! I THINK I SEE THE SCHOOL BUS! DON'T FORGET YOUR SNEAKERS AGAIN.

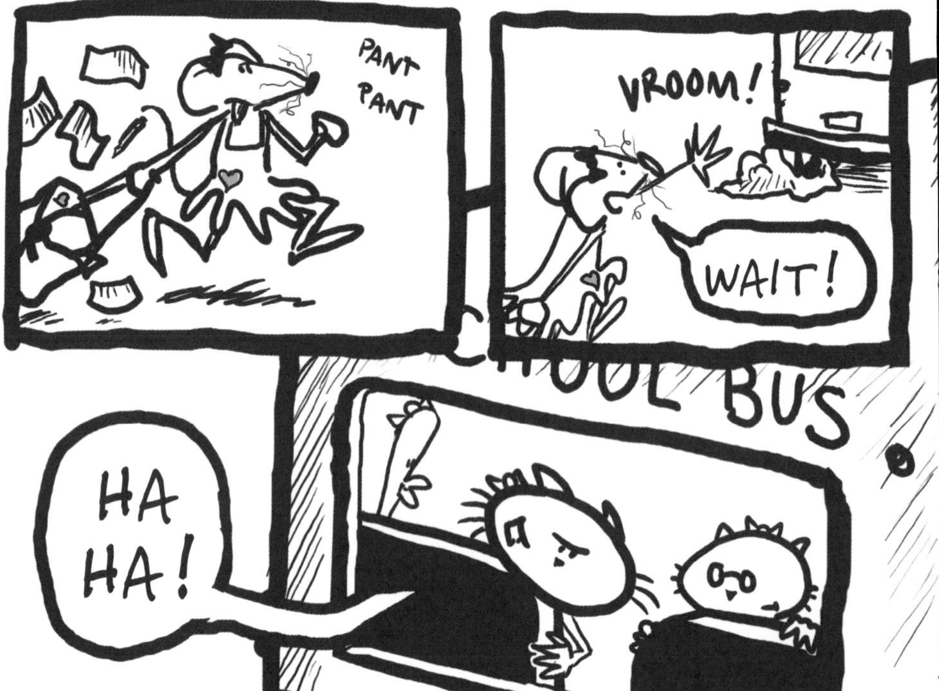
PANT
PANT
VROOM!
WAIT!
SCHOOL BUS
HA HA!
PANT
PANT
TYPICAL.
AT LEAST YOU GOT SOME EXERCISE, BABYMOUSE.

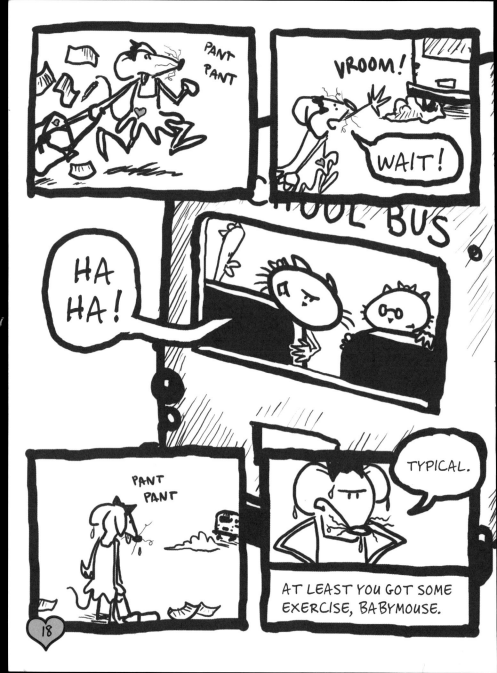

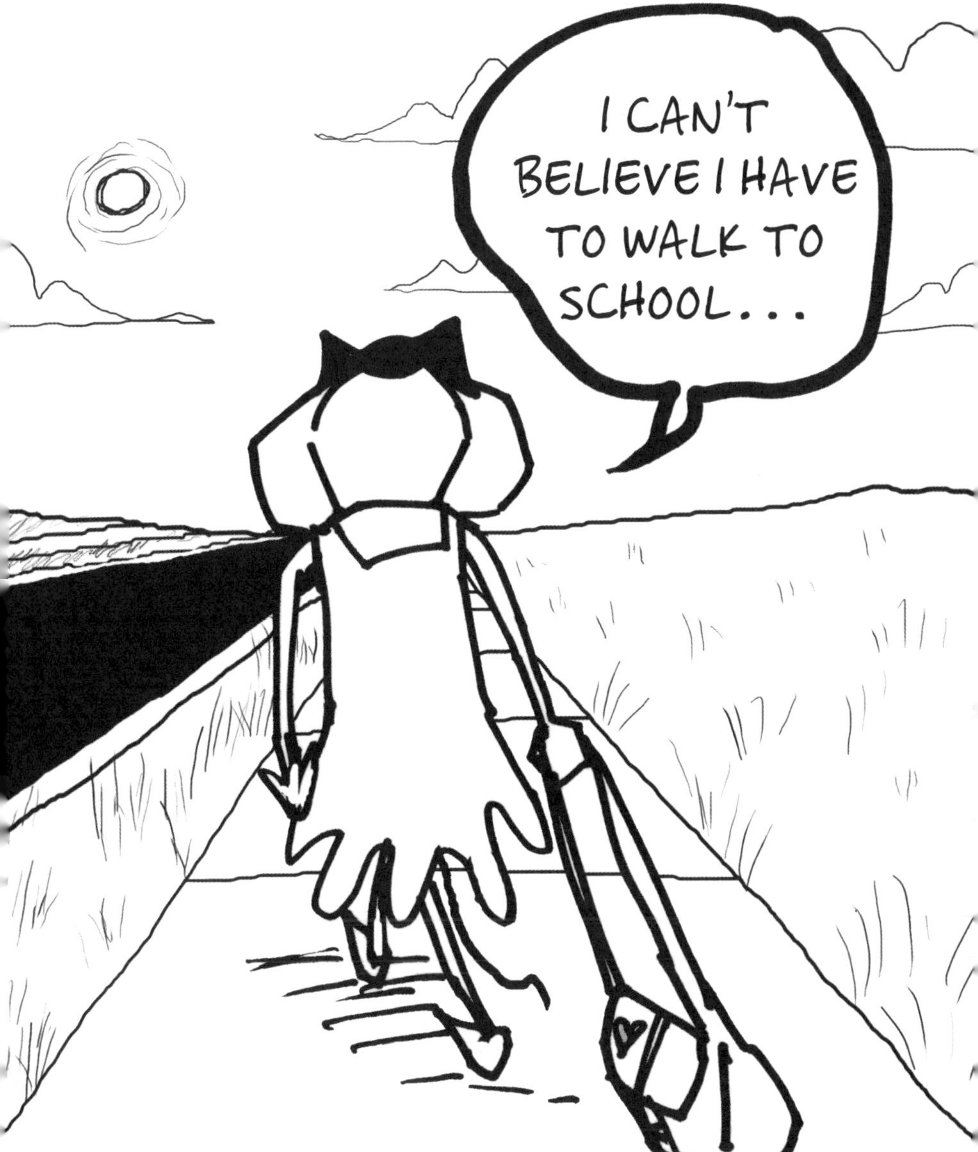
I CAN'T BELIEVE I HAVE TO WALK TO SCHOOL...

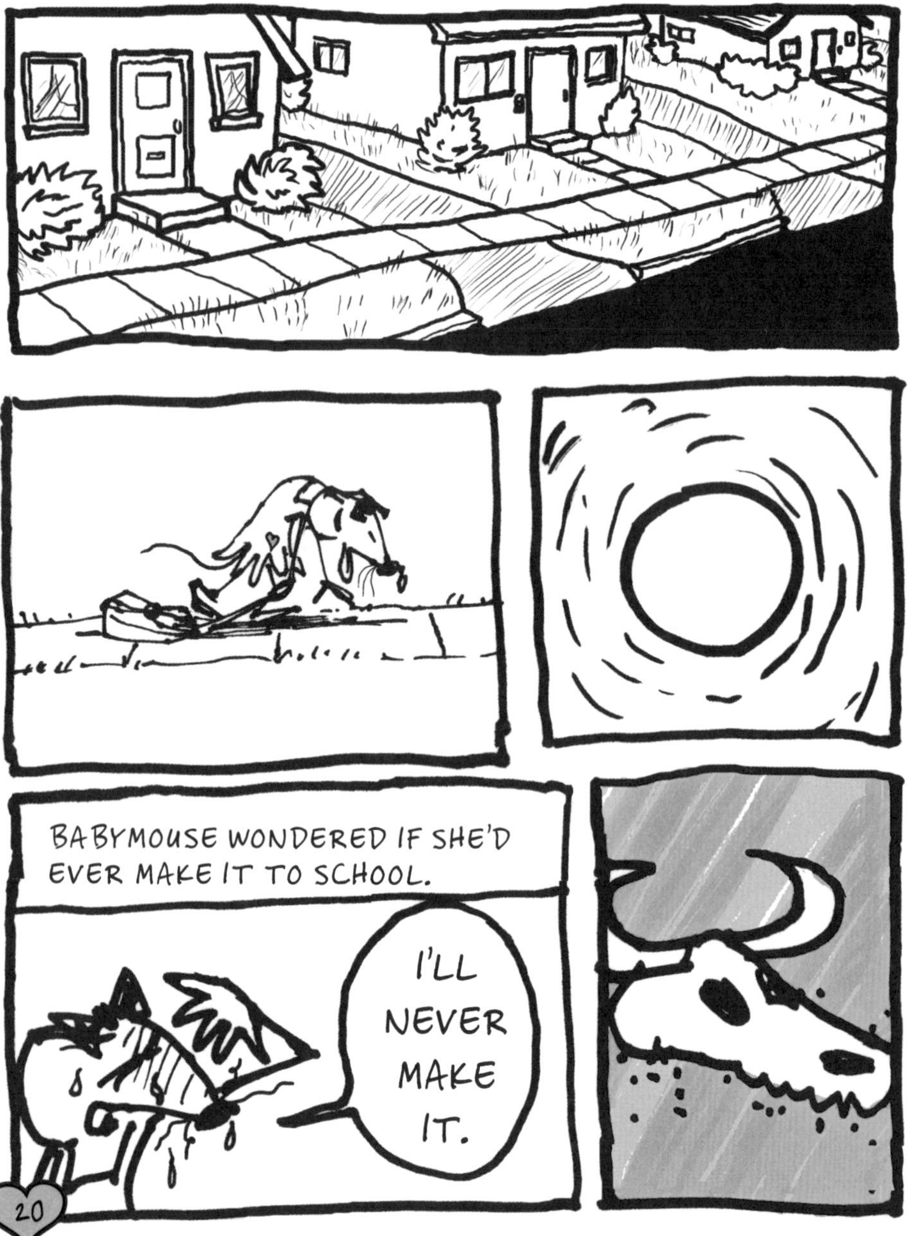
BABYMOUSE WONDERED IF SHE'D EVER MAKE IT TO SCHOOL.
I'LL NEVER MAKE IT.

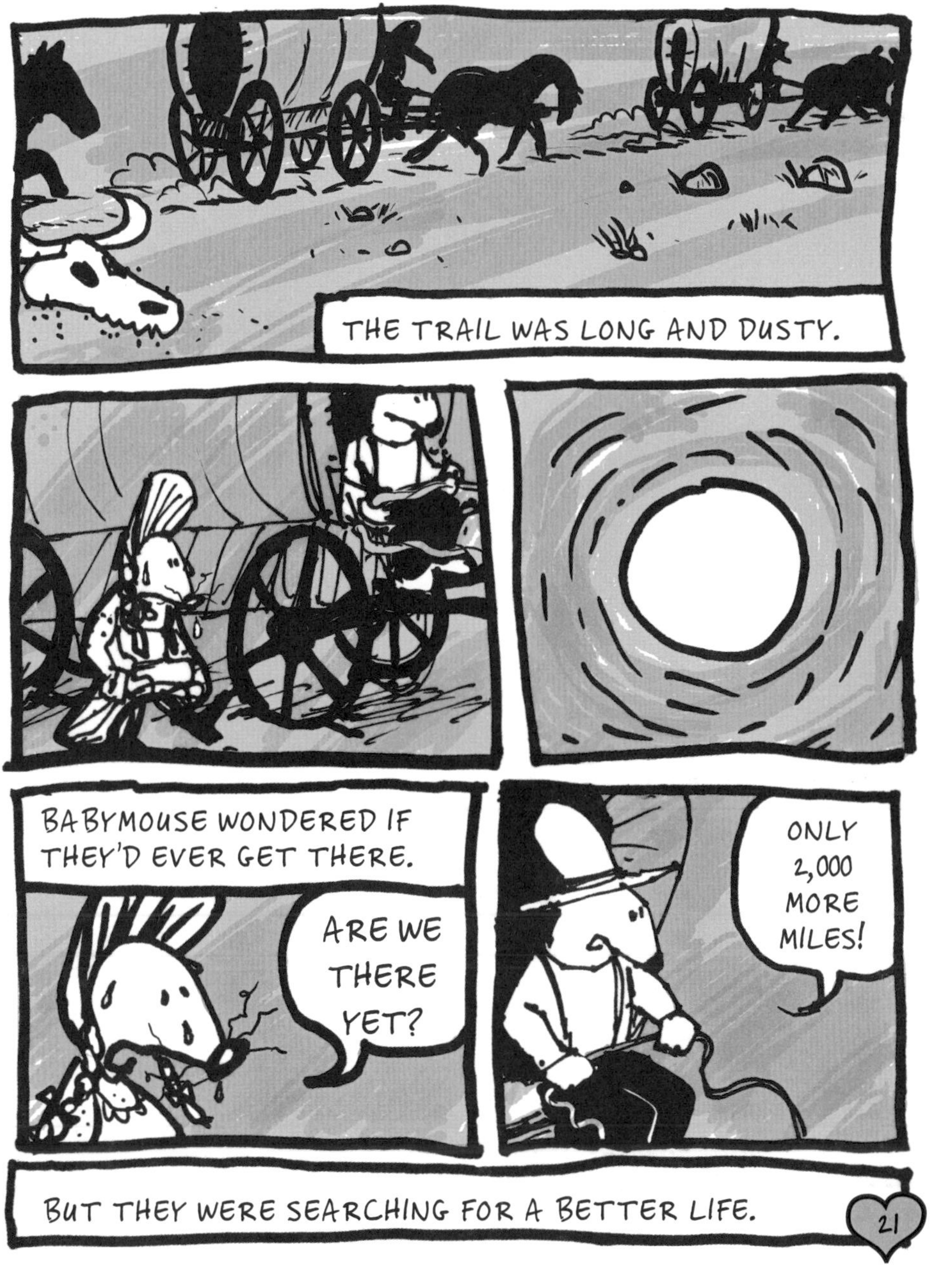
THE TRAIL WAS LONG AND DUSTY.
BABYMOUSE WONDERED IF THEY'D EVER GET THERE.
ARE WE THERE YET?
ONLY 2,000 MORE MILES!
BUT THEY WERE SEARCHING FOR A BETTER LIFE.

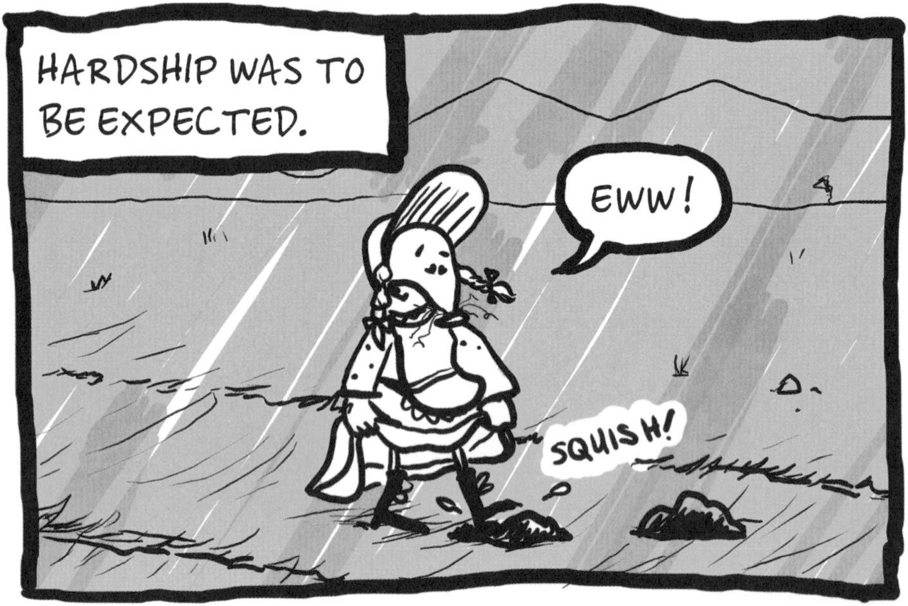
HARDSHIP WAS TO BE EXPECTED.
EWW!
SQUISH!

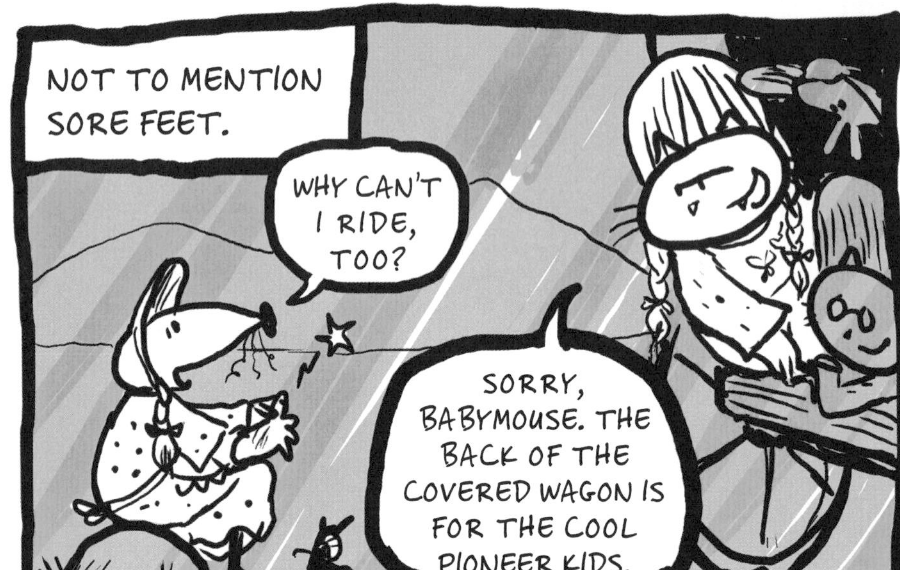
NOT TO MENTION SORE FEET.
WHY CAN'T I RIDE, TOO?
SORRY, BABYMOUSE. THE BACK OF THE COVERED WAGON IS FOR THE COOL PIONEER KIDS.

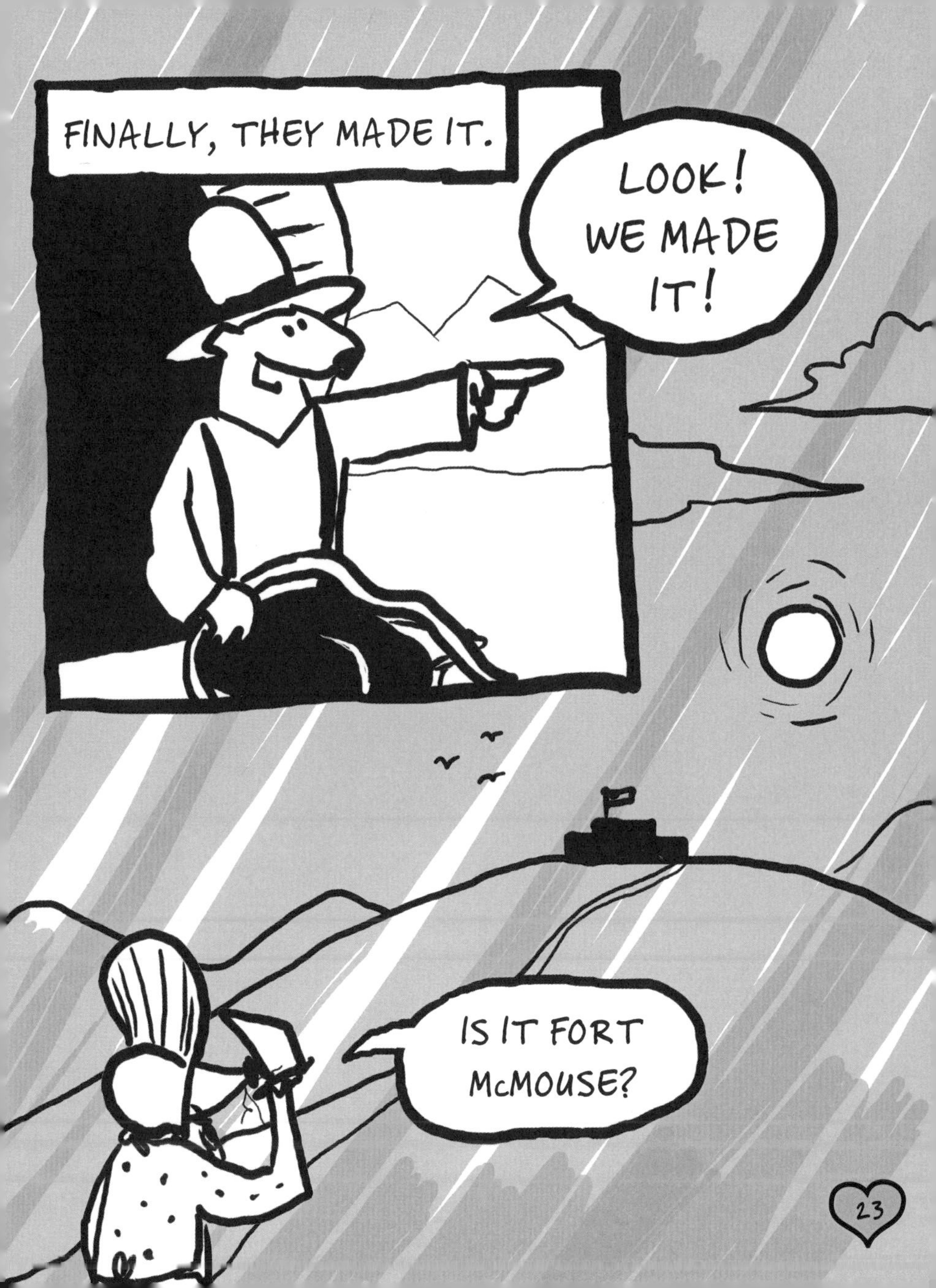
FINALLY, THEY MADE IT.
LOOK! WE MADE IT!
IS IT FORT McMOUSE?

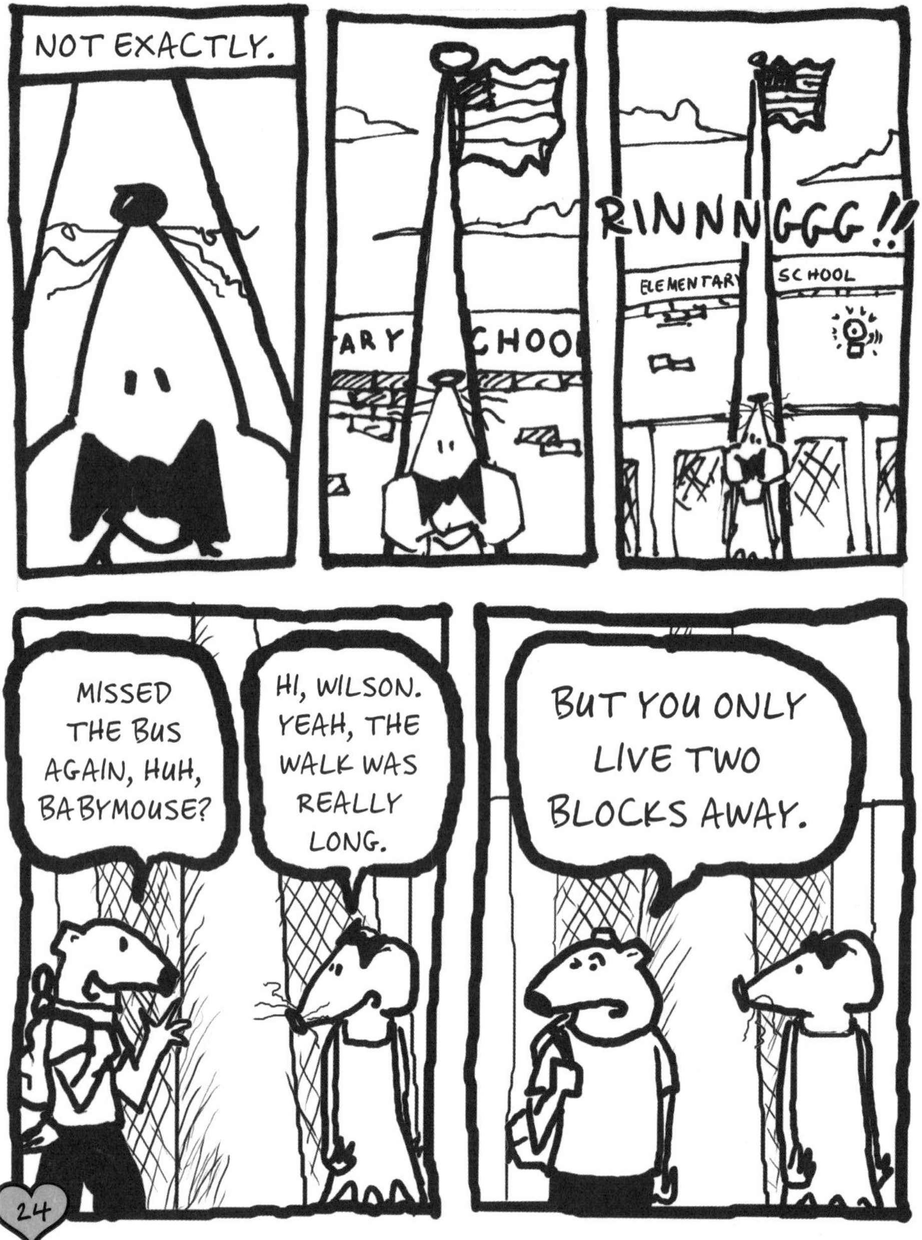
NOT EXACTLY.
ARY CHOO
RINNNGGG!!
ELEMENTARY SCHOOL
MISSED THE BUS AGAIN, HUH, BABYMOUSE?
HI, WILSON. YEAH, THE WALK WAS REALLY LONG.
BUT YOU ONLY LIVE TWO BLOCKS AWAY.

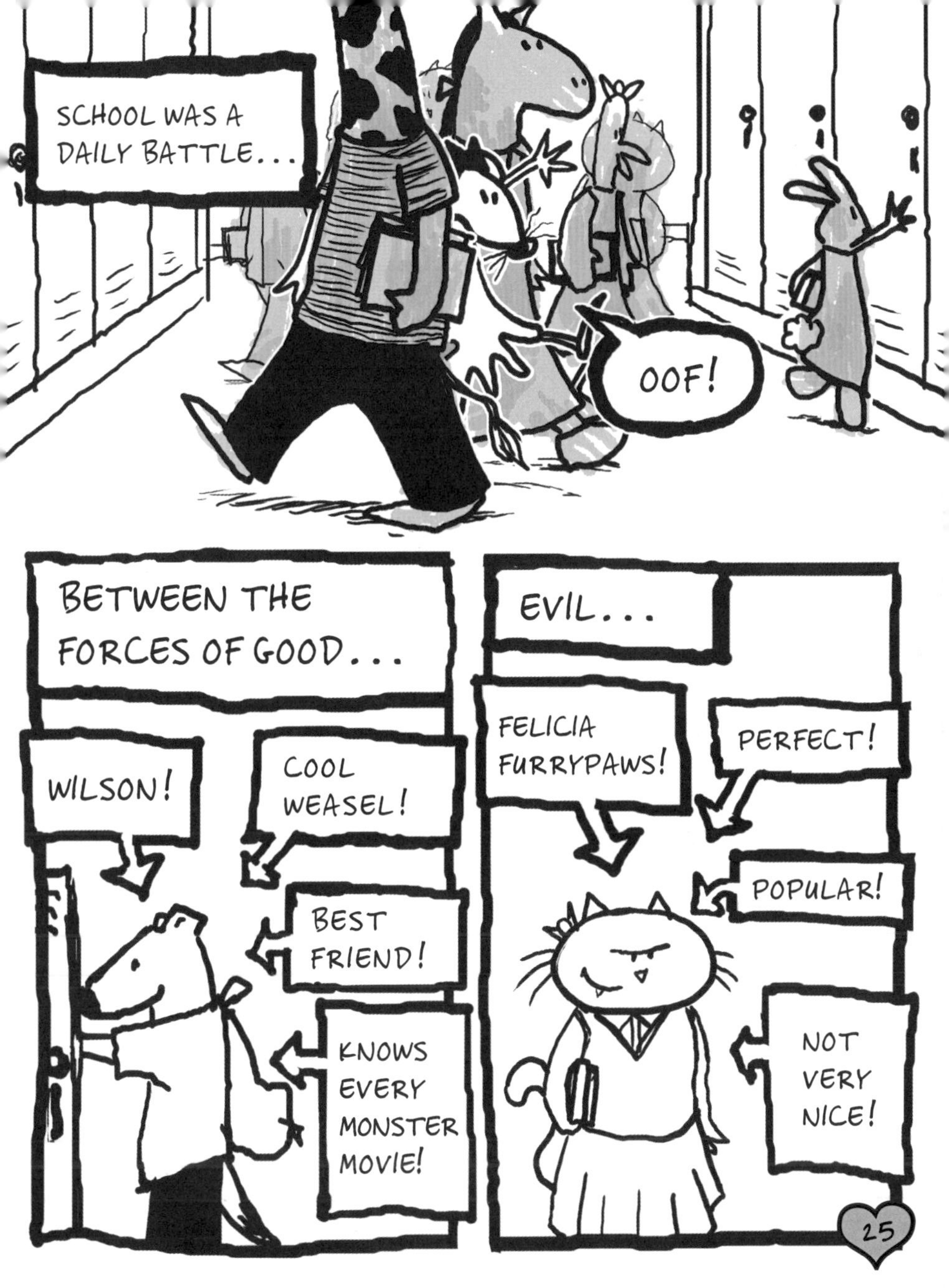
SCHOOL WAS A DAILY BATTLE...
OOF!
BETWEEN THE FORCES OF GOOD...
WILSON!
COOL WEASEL!
BEST FRIEND!
KNOWS EVERY MONSTER MOVIE!
EVIL...
FELICIA FURRYPAWS!
PERFECT!
POPULAR!
NOT VERY NICE!

...AND LOCKER!

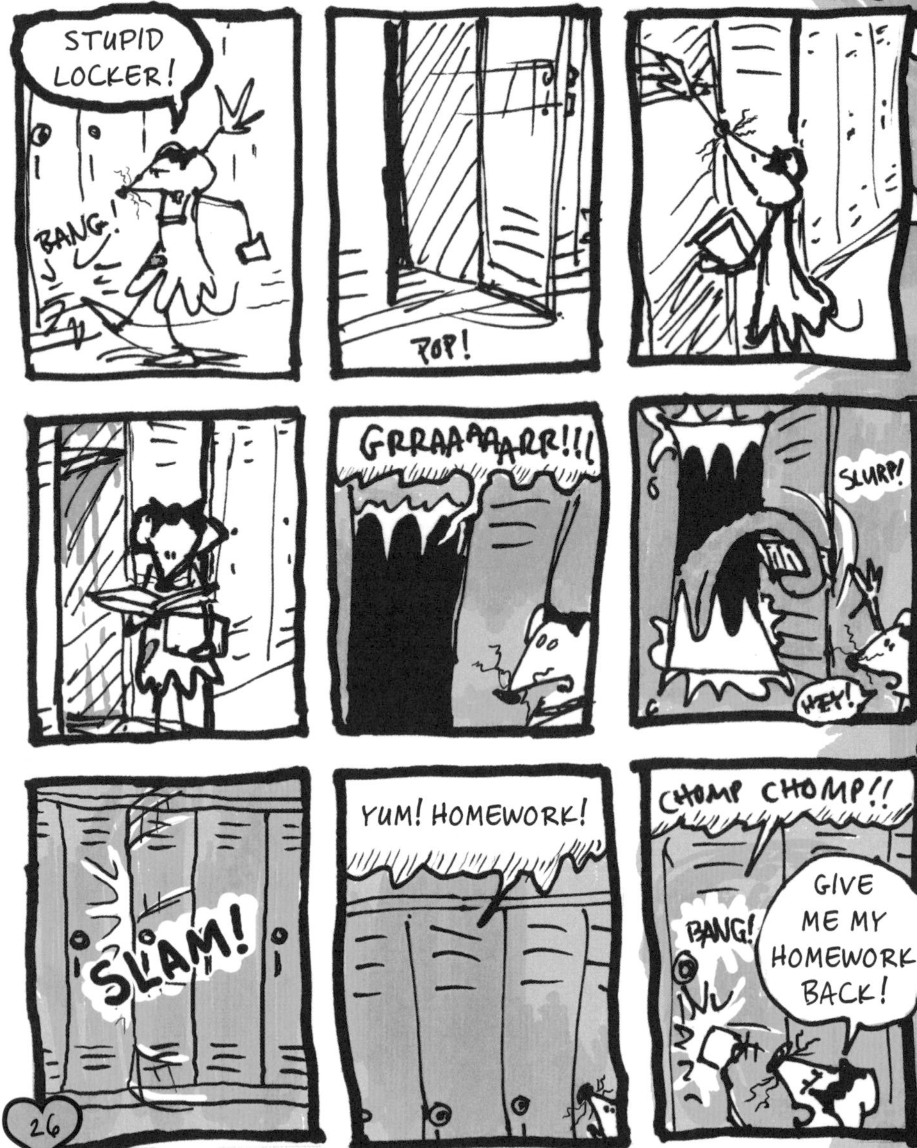

STUPID LOCKER!
BANG!
POP!
GRRAAAAARR!!!
SLURP!
HEY!
SLAM!
YUM! HOMEWORK!
CHOMP CHOMP!!
BANG!
GIVE ME MY HOMEWORK BACK!

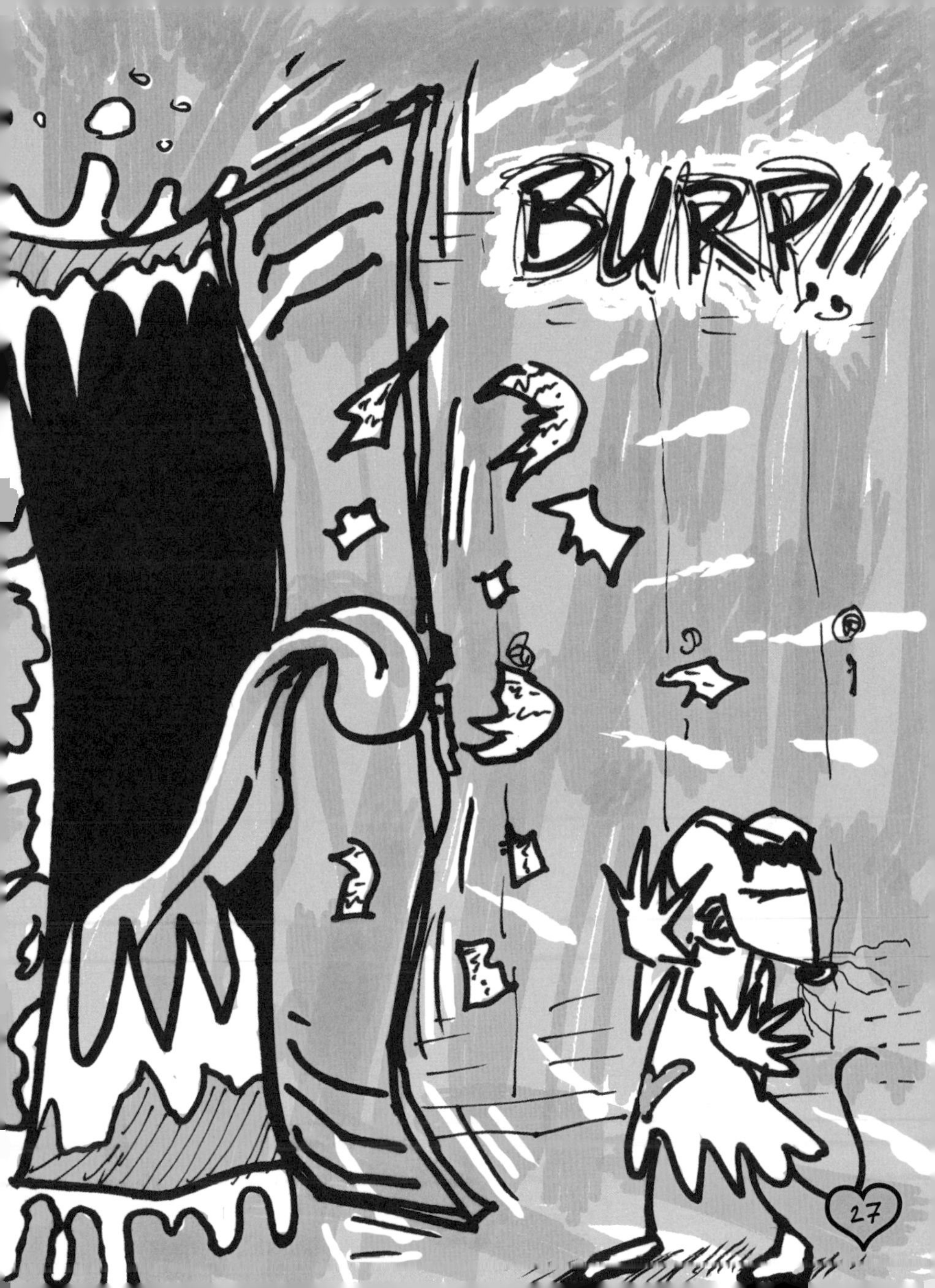
BURP!!

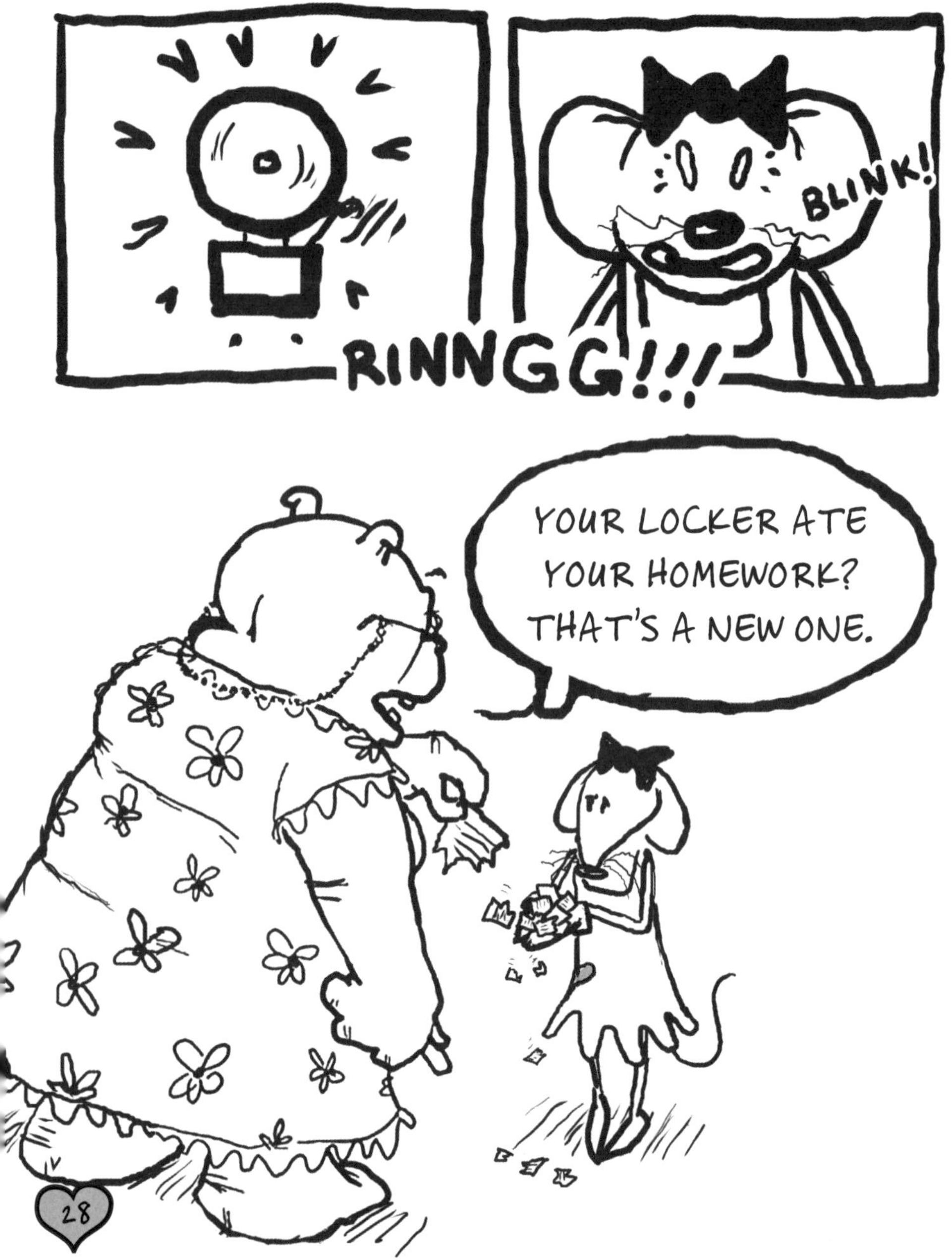
RINNGG!!!
BLINK!
YOUR LOCKER ATE YOUR HOMEWORK? THAT'S A NEW ONE.

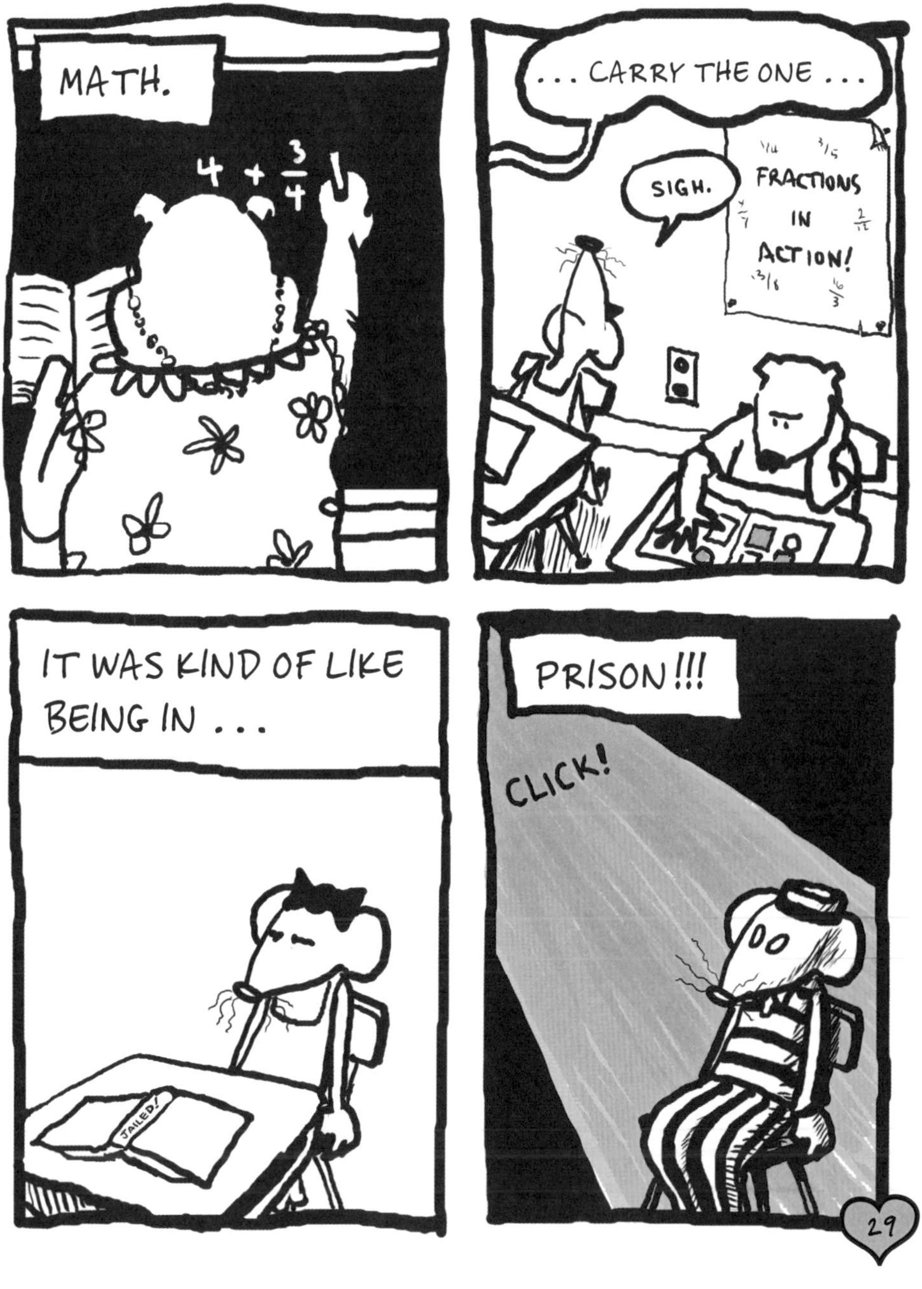
MATH.
4 + 3/4
... CARRY THE ONE ...
SIGH.
FRACTIONS IN ACTION!
IT WAS KIND OF LIKE BEING IN ...
JAILED!
PRISON!!!
CLICK!

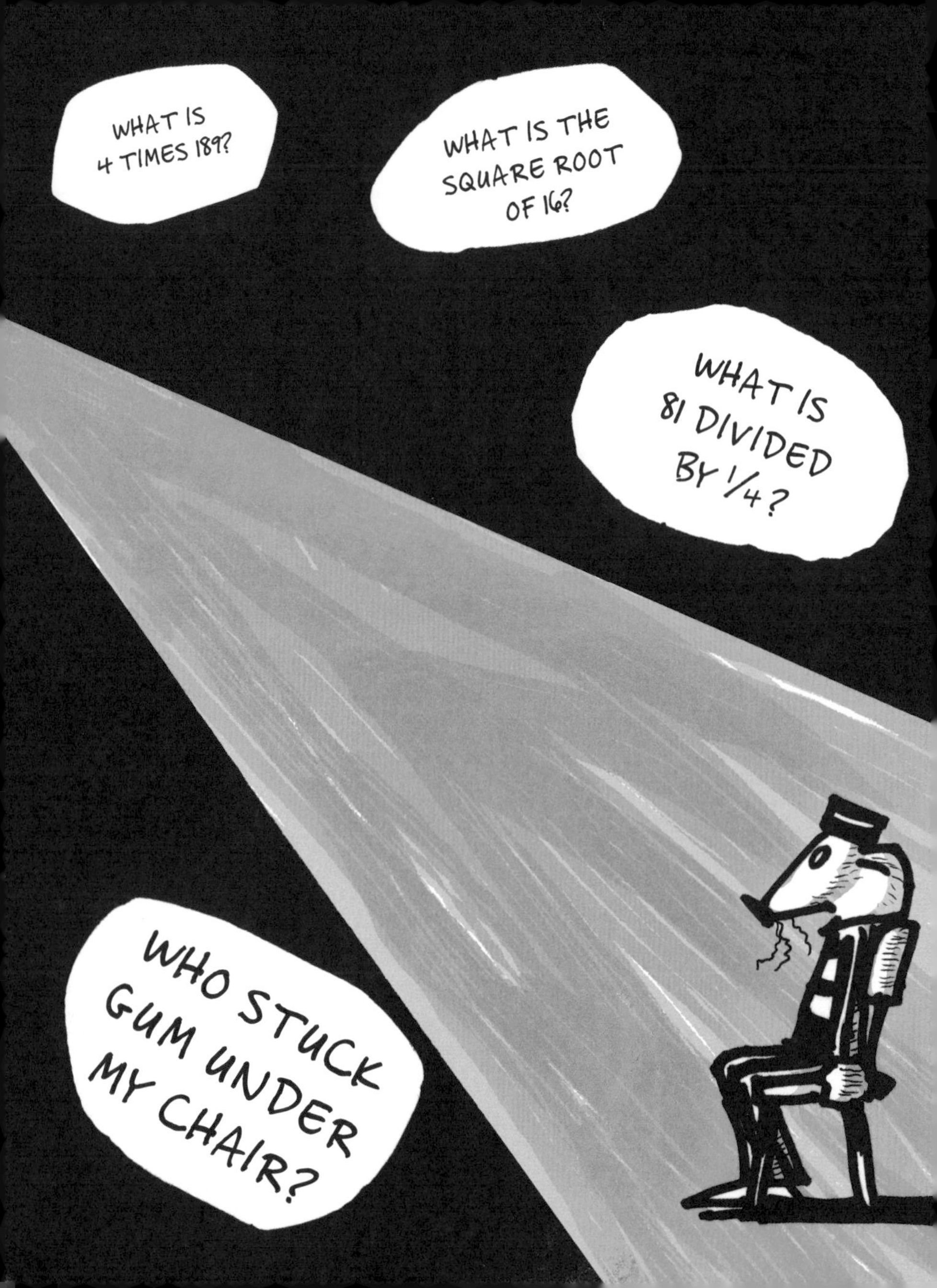
WHAT IS 4 TIMES 189?
WHAT IS THE SQUARE ROOT OF 16?
WHAT IS 81 DIVIDED BY 1/4?
WHO STUCK GUM UNDER MY CHAIR?

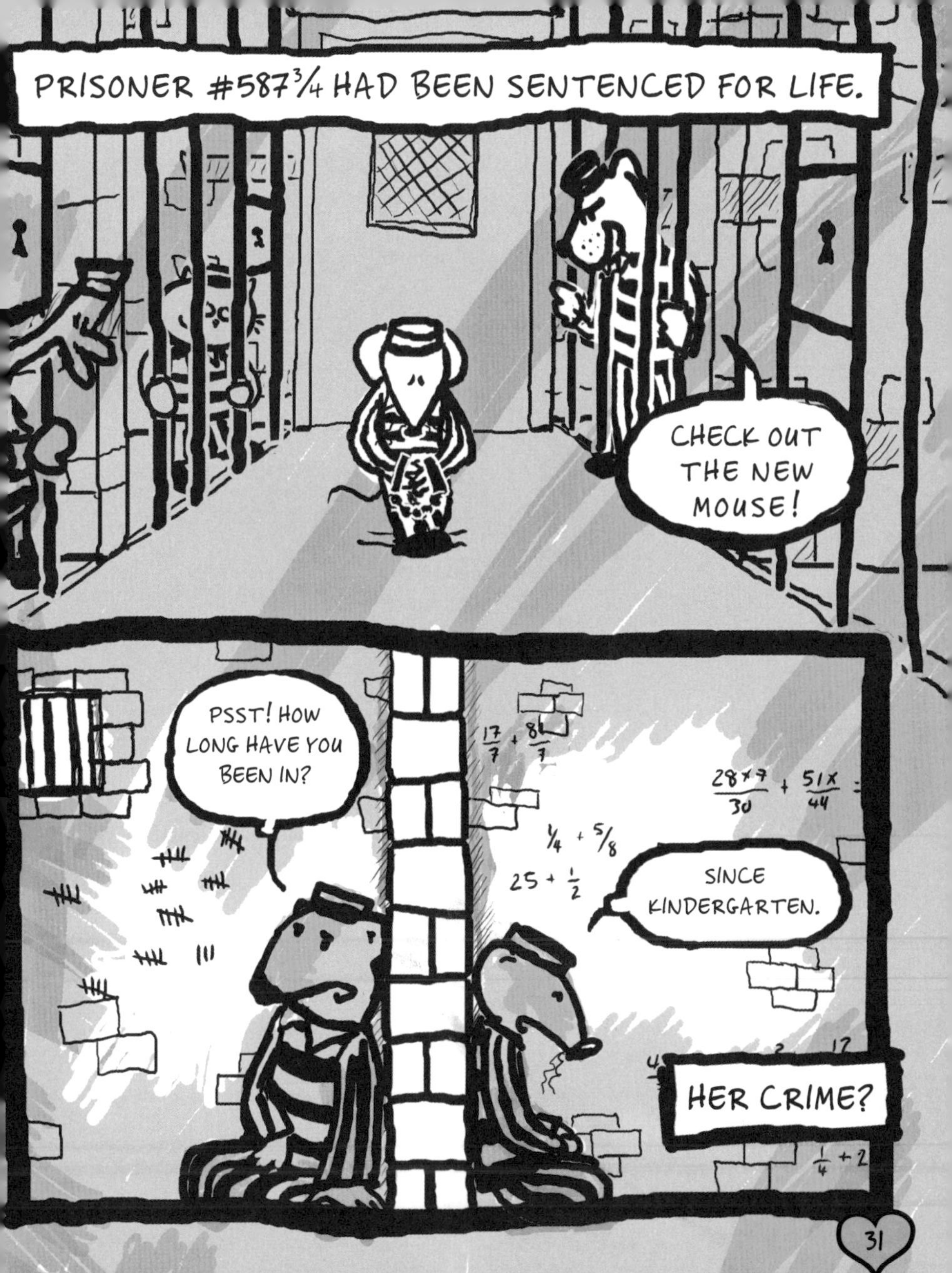
PRISONER #587¾ HAD BEEN SENTENCED FOR LIFE.
CHECK OUT THE NEW MOUSE!
PSST! HOW LONG HAVE YOU BEEN IN?
SINCE KINDERGARTEN.
HER CRIME?

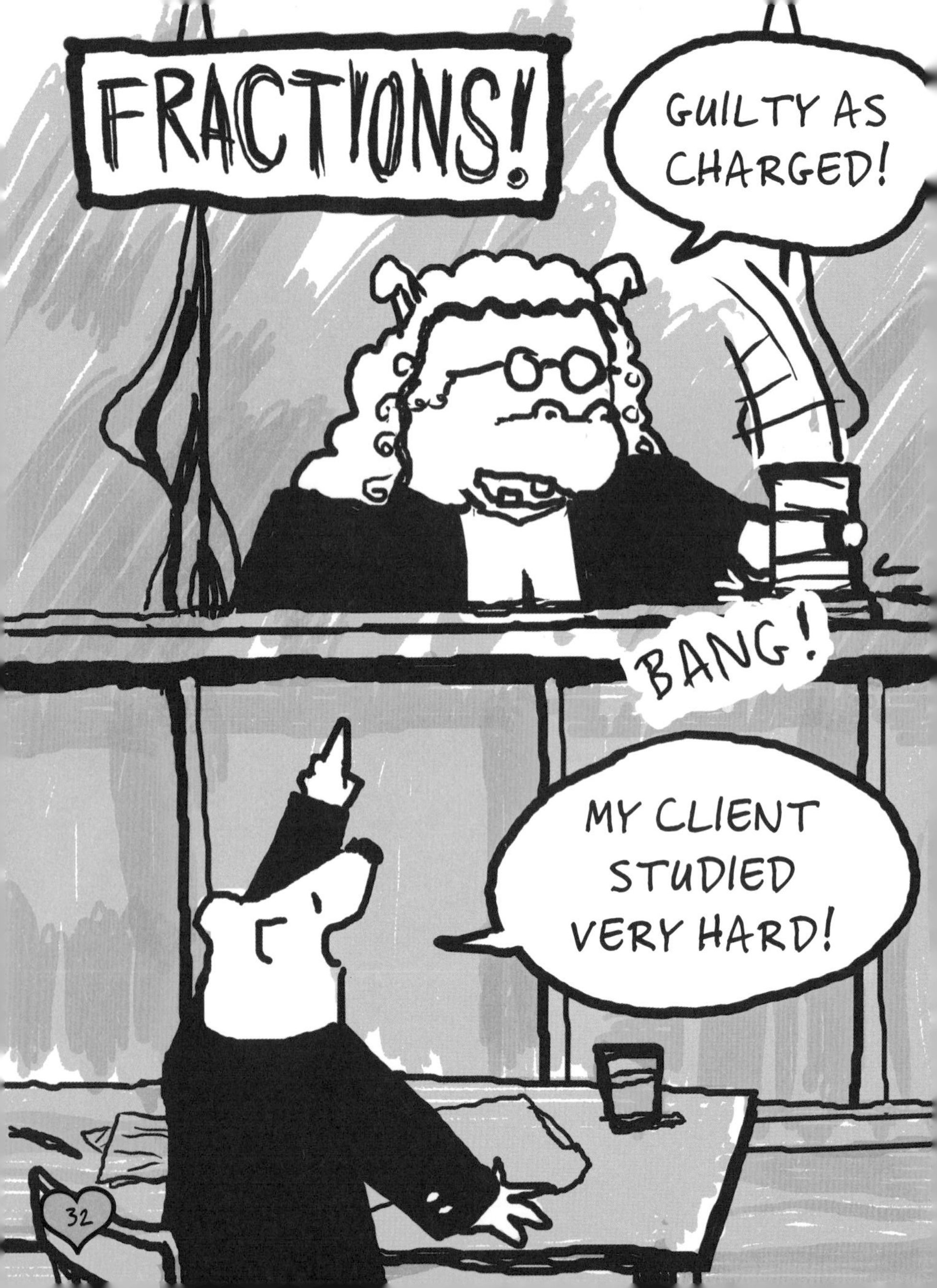
FRACTIONS!
GUILTY AS CHARGED!
BANG!
MY CLIENT STUDIED VERY HARD!

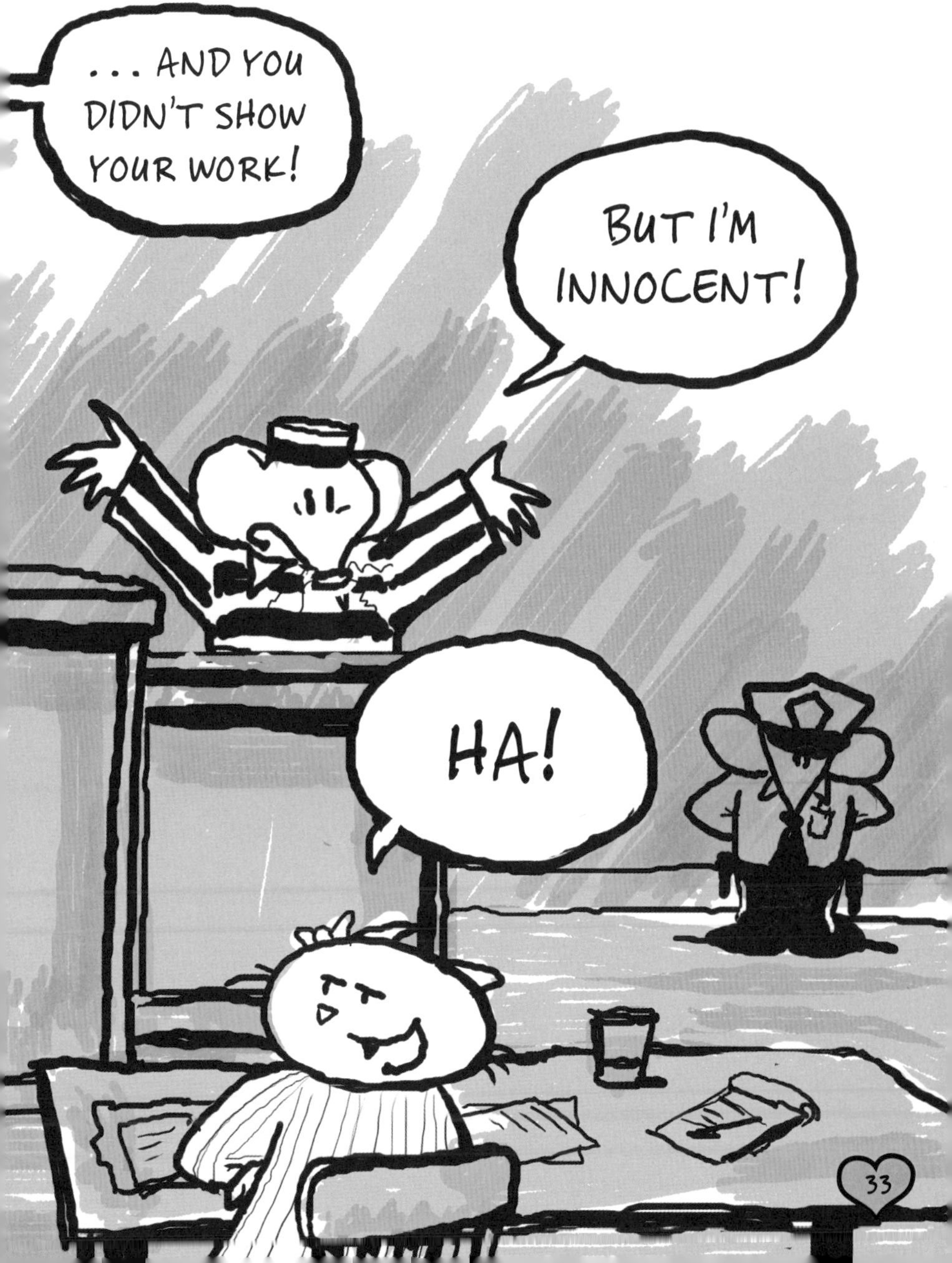
. . . AND YOU DIDN'T SHOW YOUR WORK!
BUT I'M INNOCENT!
HA!

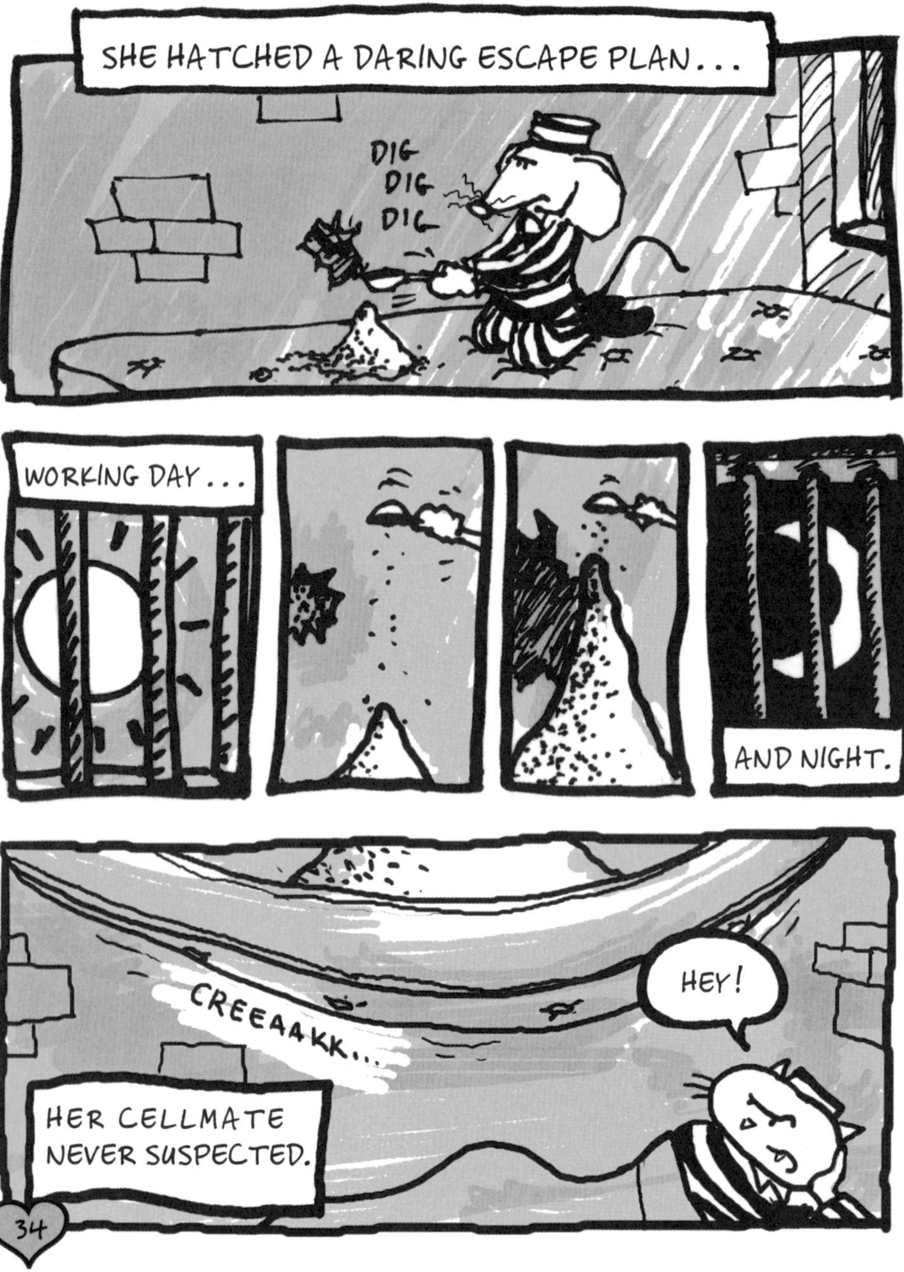
SHE HATCHED A DARING ESCAPE PLAN...
DIG
DIG
DIG
WORKING DAY...
AND NIGHT.
CREEAAKK...
HEY!
HER CELLMATE NEVER SUSPECTED.

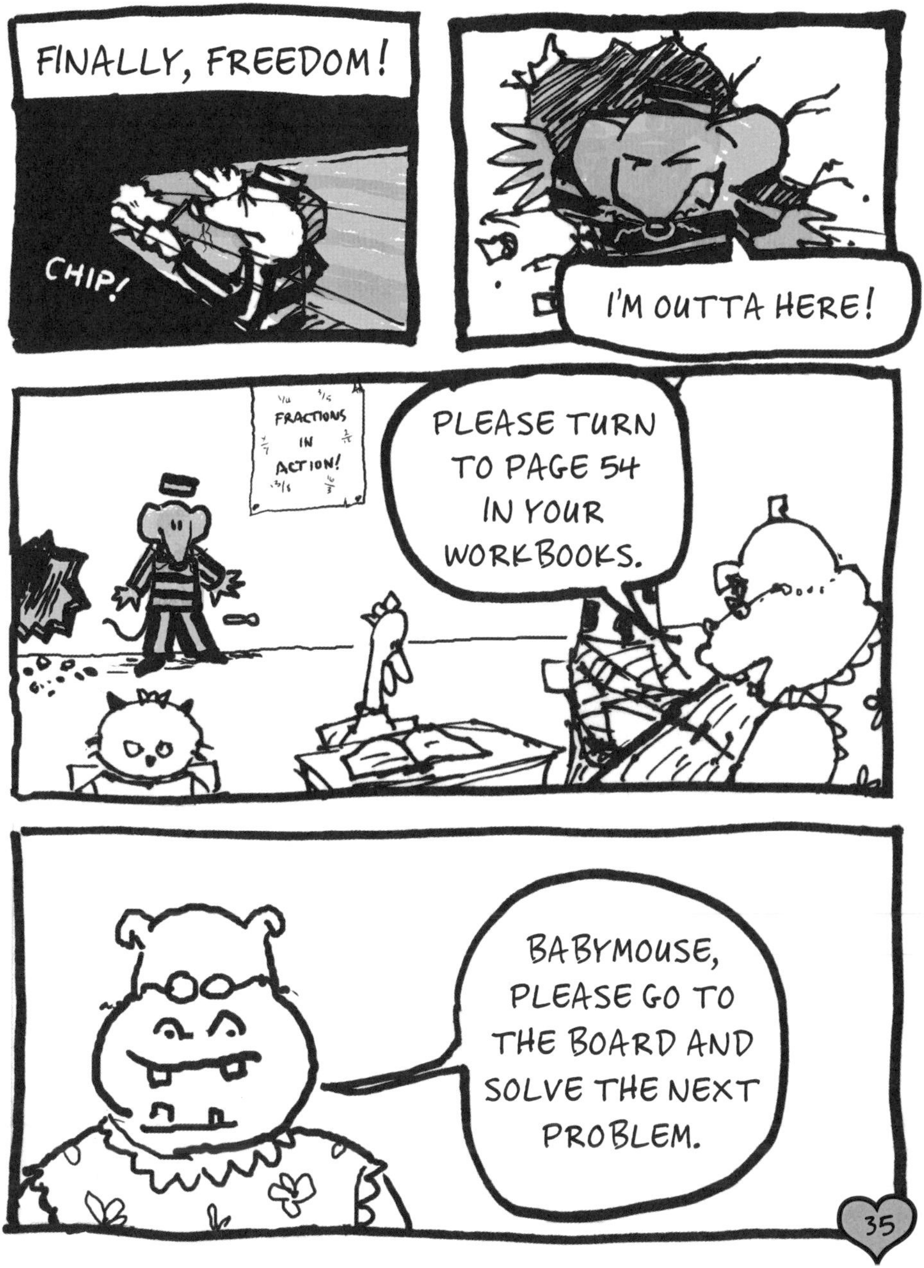
FINALLY, FREEDOM!
CHIP!
I'M OUTTA HERE!
FRACTIONS IN ACTION!
PLEASE TURN TO PAGE 54 IN YOUR WORKBOOKS.
BABYMOUSE, PLEASE GO TO THE BOARD AND SOLVE THE NEXT PROBLEM.

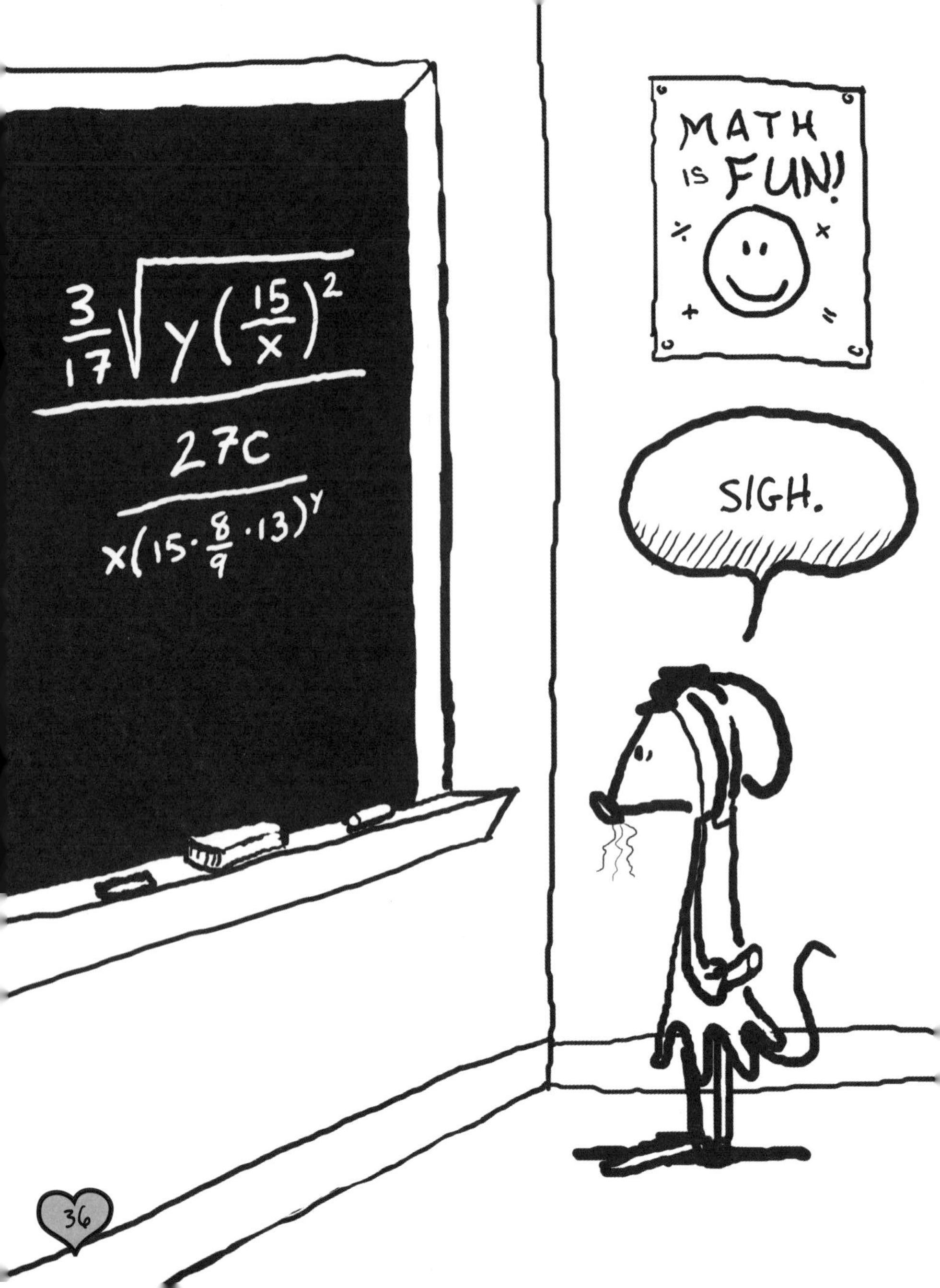
MATH IS FUN!
SIGH.

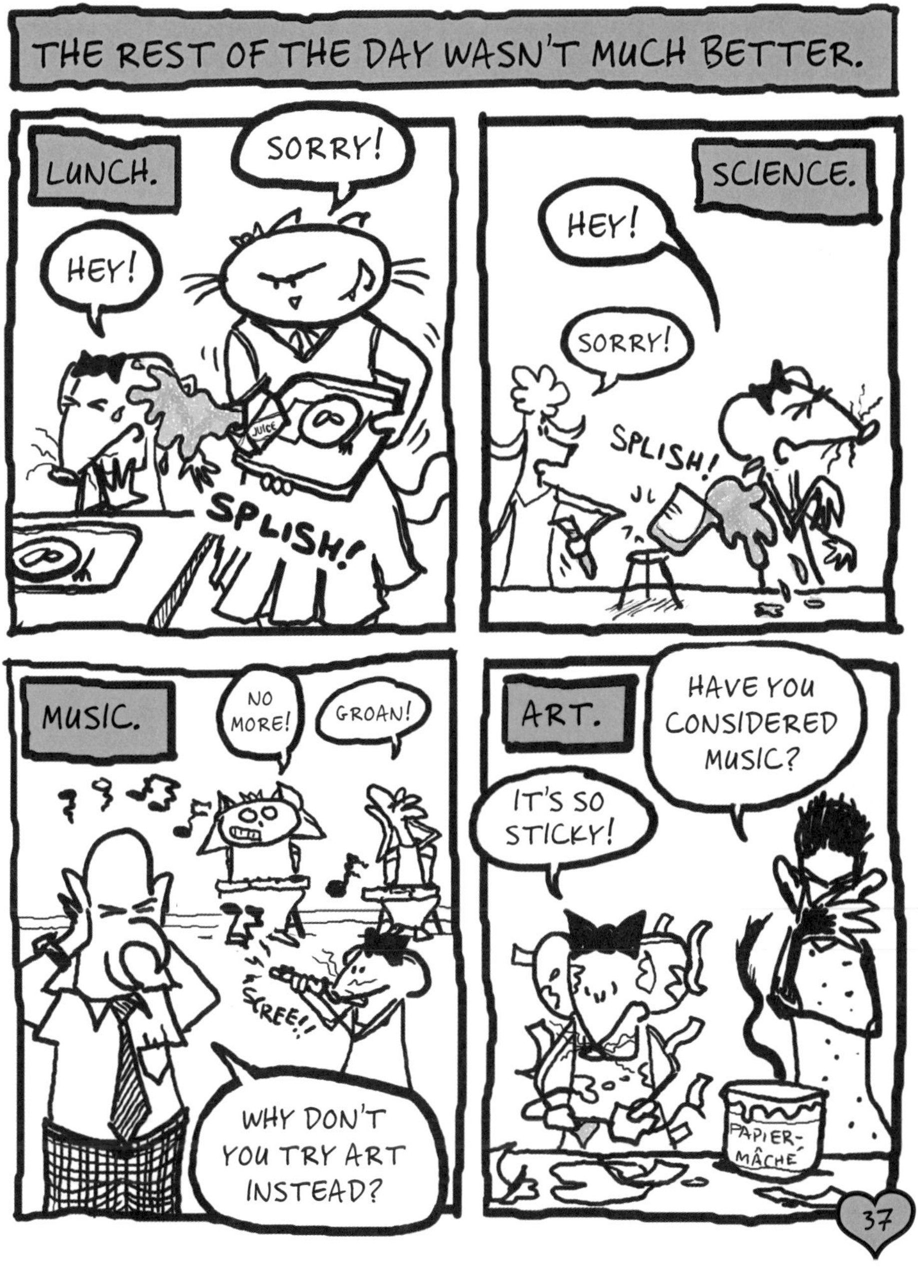
THE REST OF THE DAY WASN'T MUCH BETTER.
LUNCH.
HEY!
SORRY!
JUICE
SPLISH!
SCIENCE.
HEY!
SORRY!
SPLISH!
MUSIC.
NO MORE!
GROAN!
SCREE!!
WHY DON'T YOU TRY ART INSTEAD?
ART.
HAVE YOU CONSIDERED MUSIC?
IT'S SO STICKY!
PAPIER-MÂCHÉ

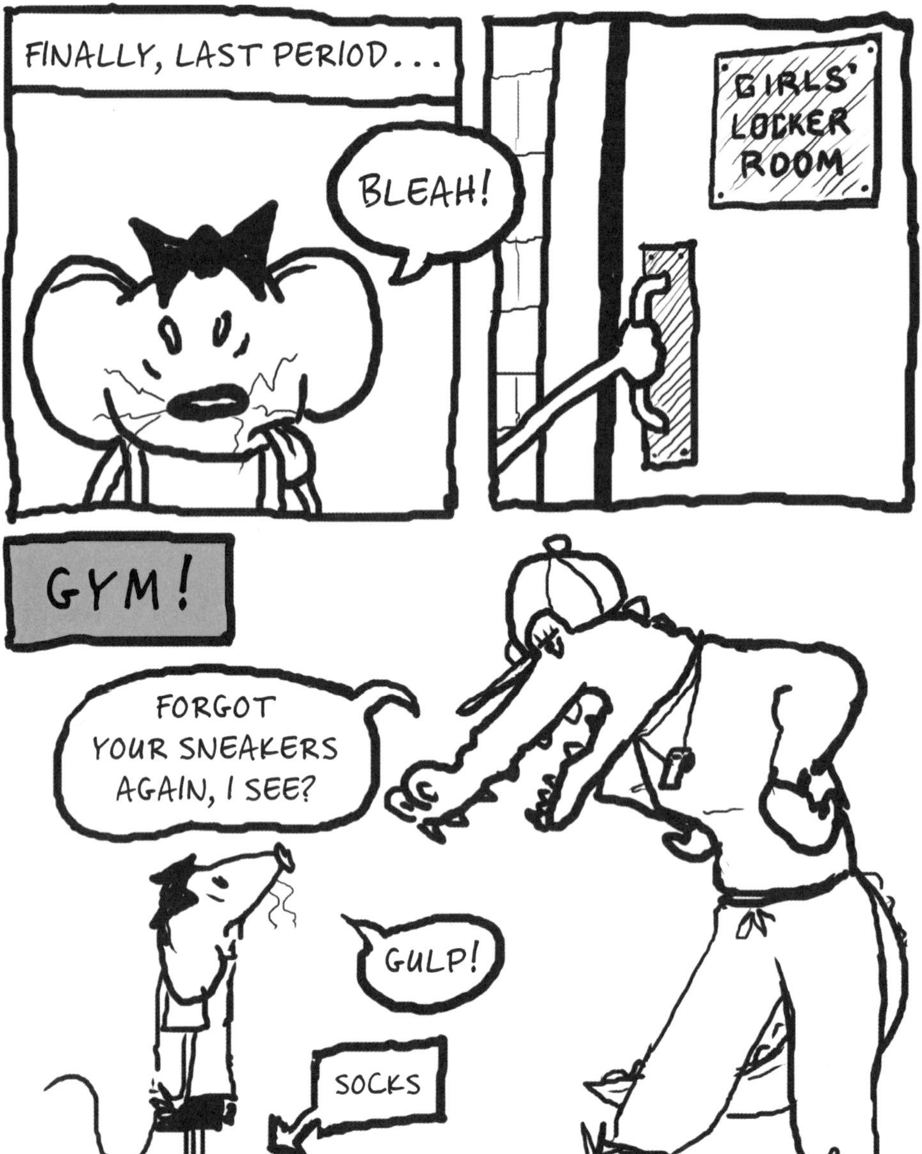
FINALLY, LAST PERIOD...
BLEAH!
GIRLS' LOCKER ROOM
GYM!
FORGOT YOUR SNEAKERS AGAIN, I SEE?
GULP!
SOCKS

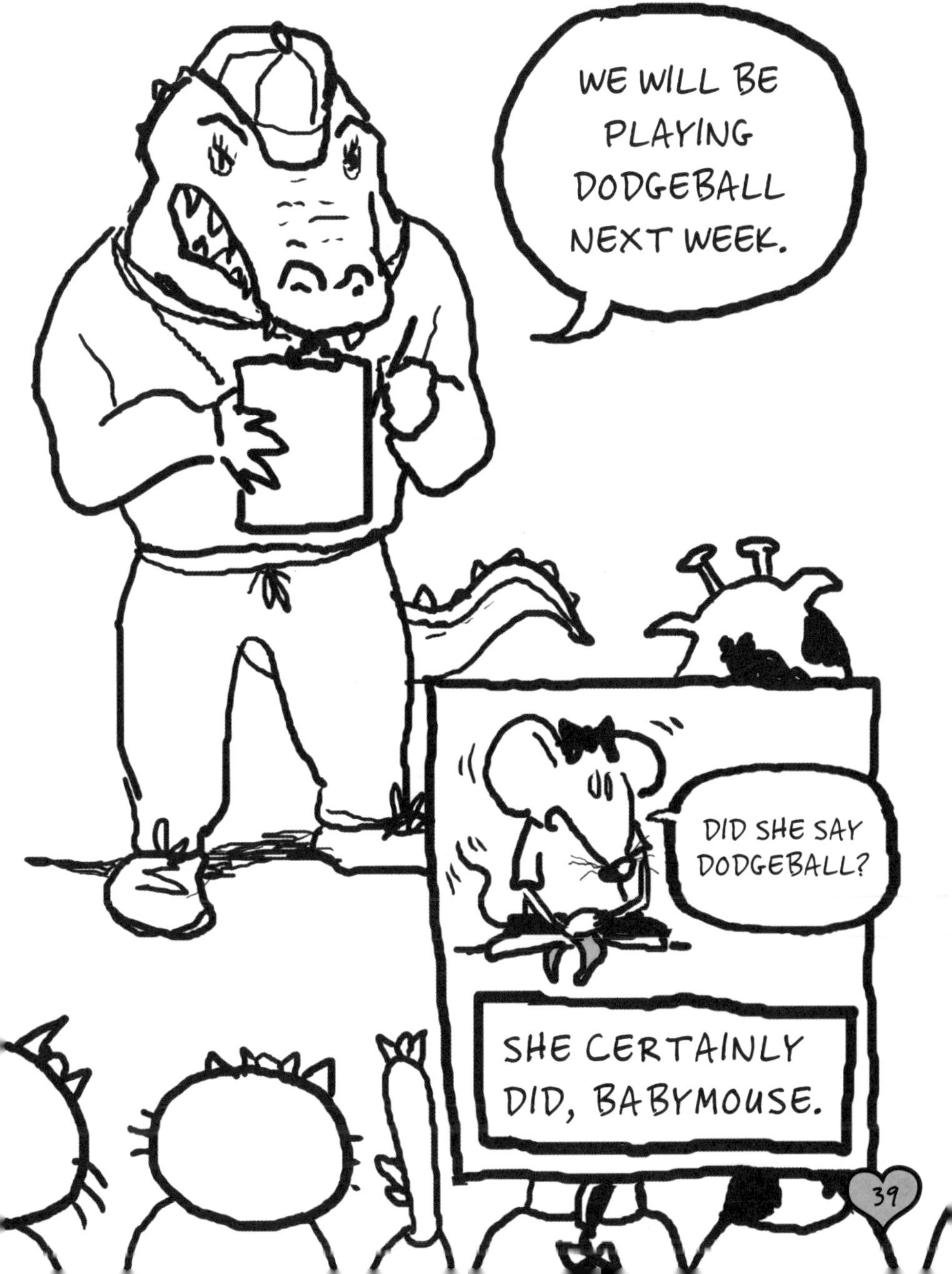
WE WILL BE PLAYING DODGEBALL NEXT WEEK.
DID SHE SAY DODGEBALL?
SHE CERTAINLY DID, BABYMOUSE.

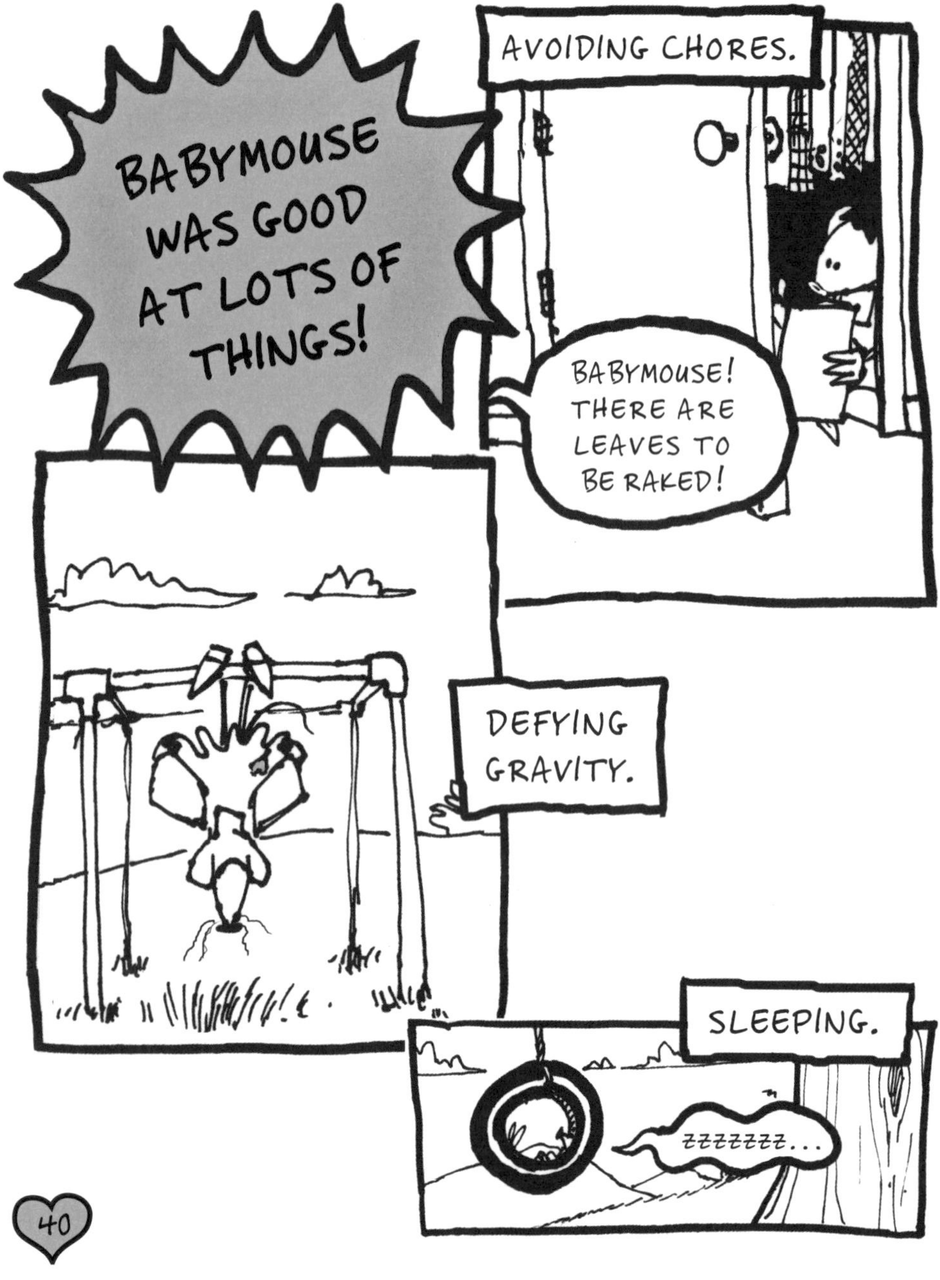
BABYMOUSE WAS GOOD AT LOTS OF THINGS!
AVOIDING CHORES.
BABYMOUSE! THERE ARE LEAVES TO BE RAKED!
DEFYING GRAVITY.
SLEEPING.
ZZZZZZZ...

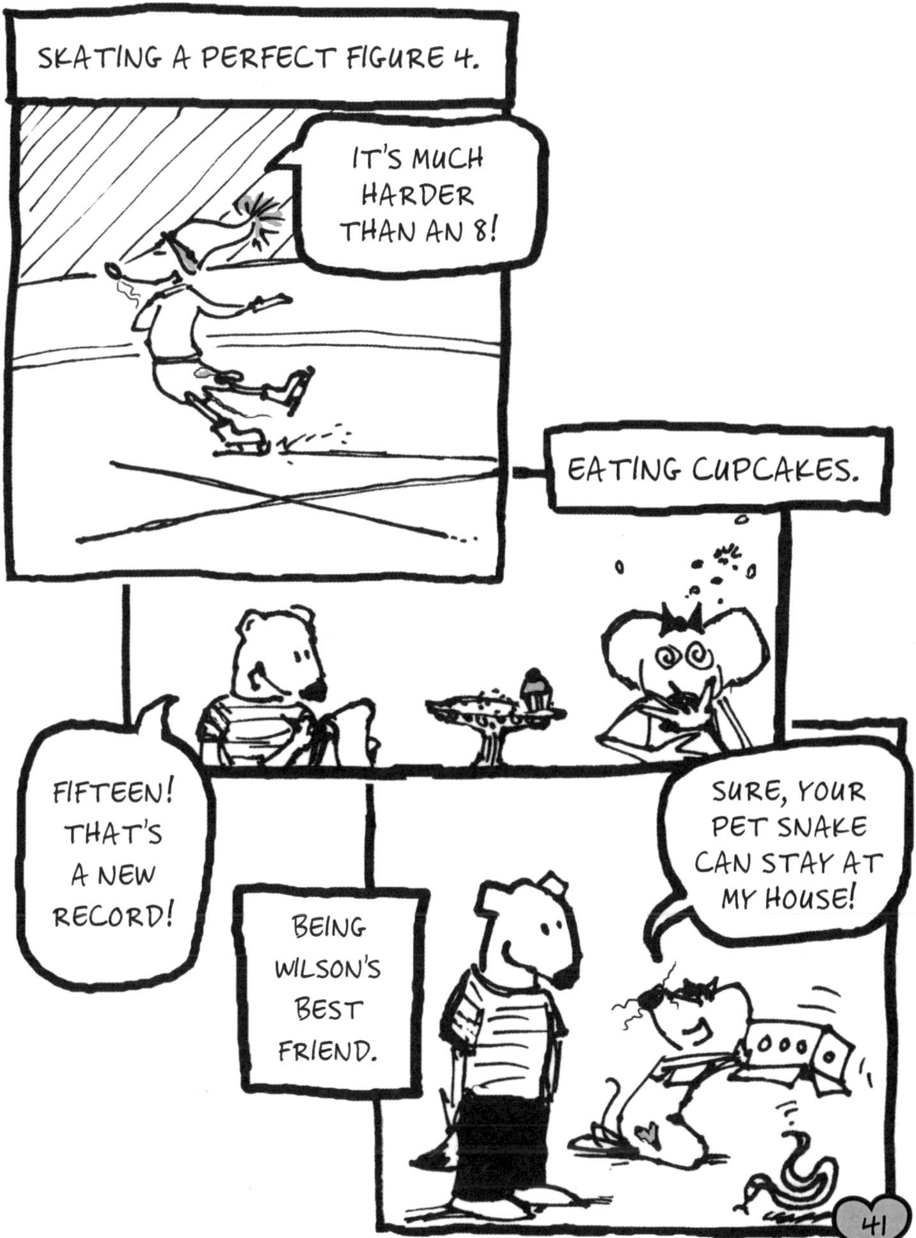
SKATING A PERFECT FIGURE 4.
IT'S MUCH HARDER THAN AN 8!
EATING CUPCAKES.
FIFTEEN! THAT'S A NEW RECORD!
BEING WILSON'S BEST FRIEND.
SURE, YOUR PET SNAKE CAN STAY AT MY HOUSE!

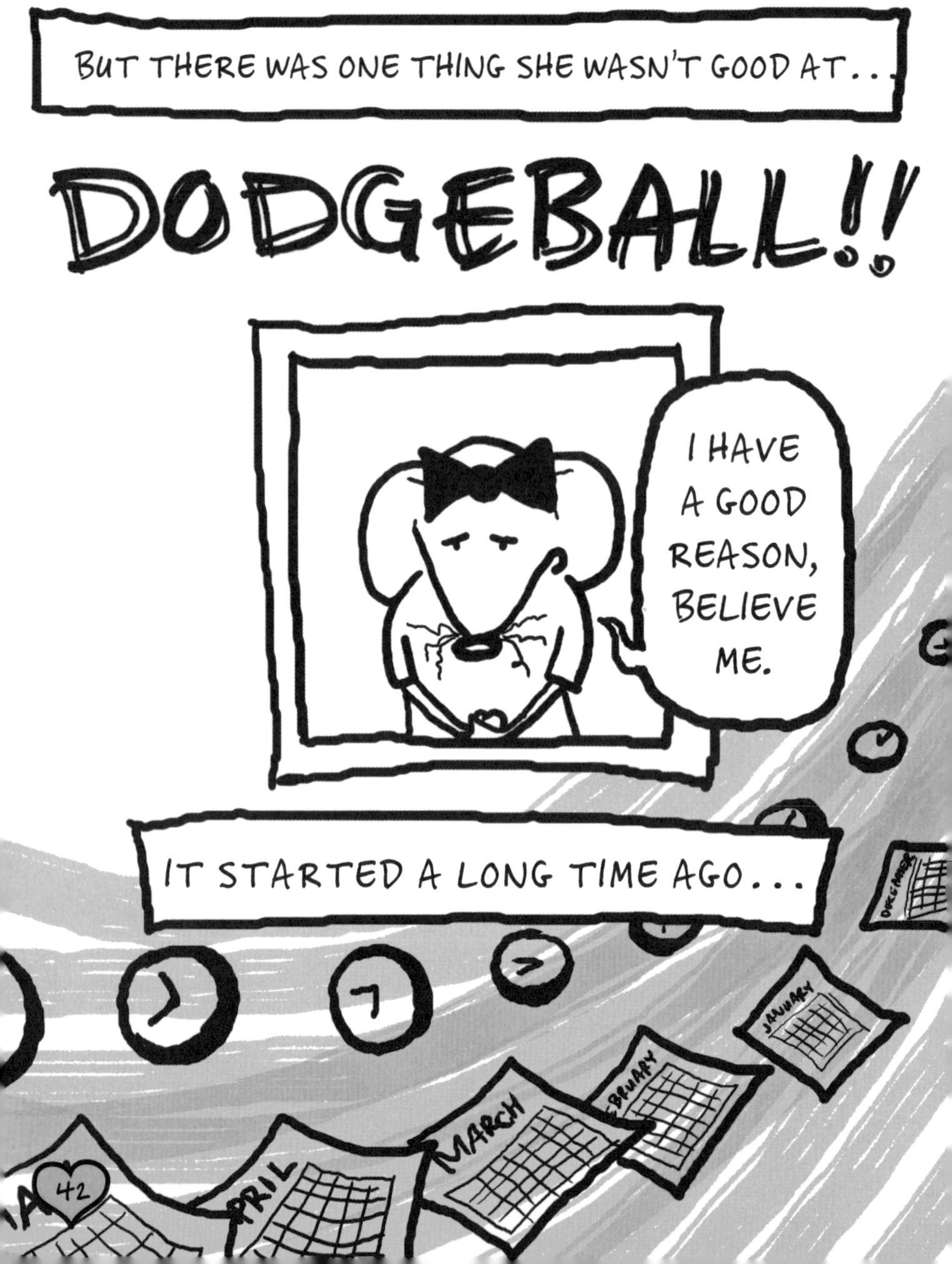
BUT THERE WAS ONE THING SHE WASN'T GOOD AT...
DODGEBALL!!
I HAVE A GOOD REASON, BELIEVE ME.
IT STARTED A LONG TIME AGO...
JANUARY
MARCH

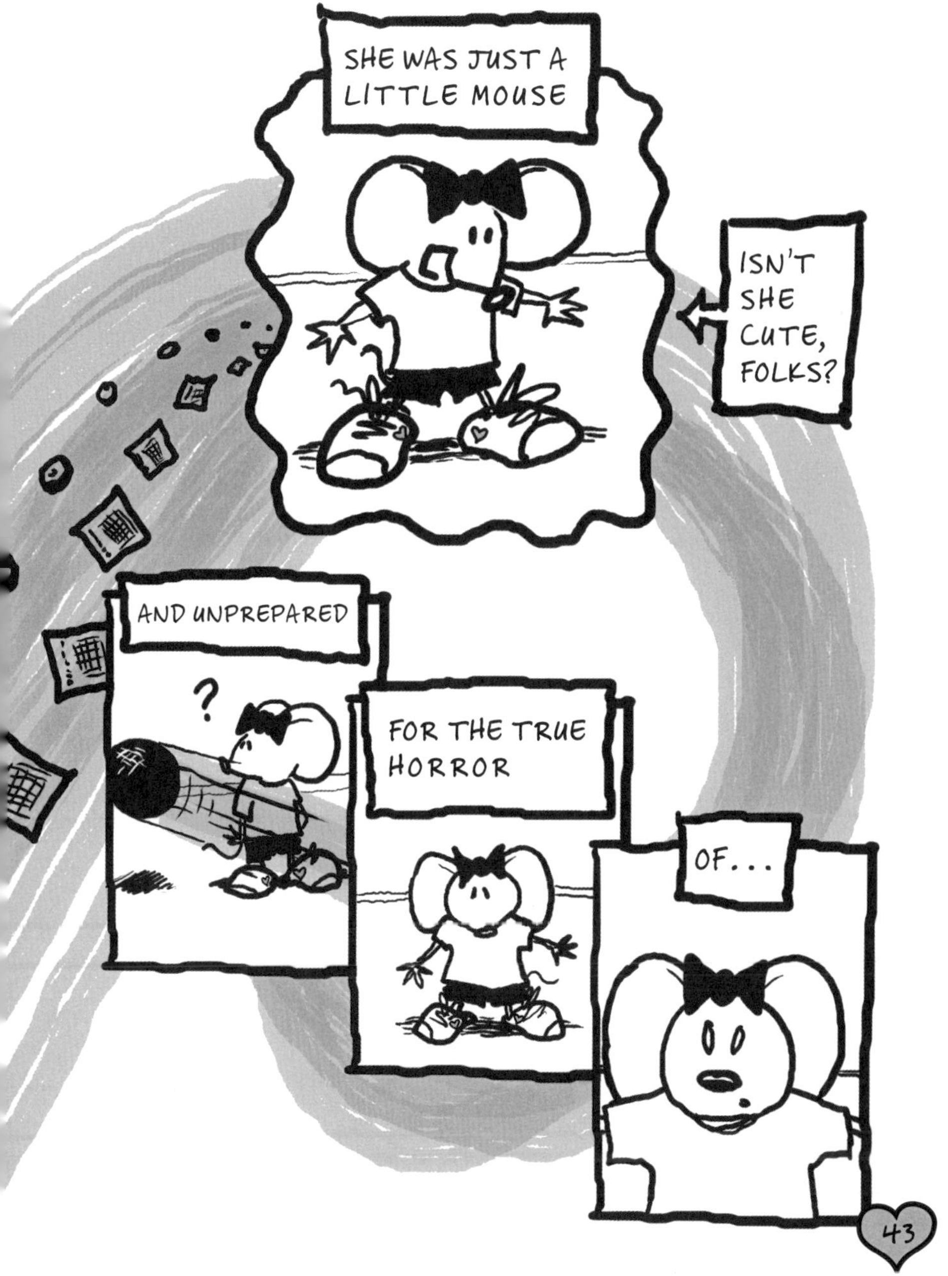
SHE WAS JUST A LITTLE MOUSE
ISN'T SHE CUTE, FOLKS?
AND UNPREPARED
?
FOR THE TRUE HORROR
OF...

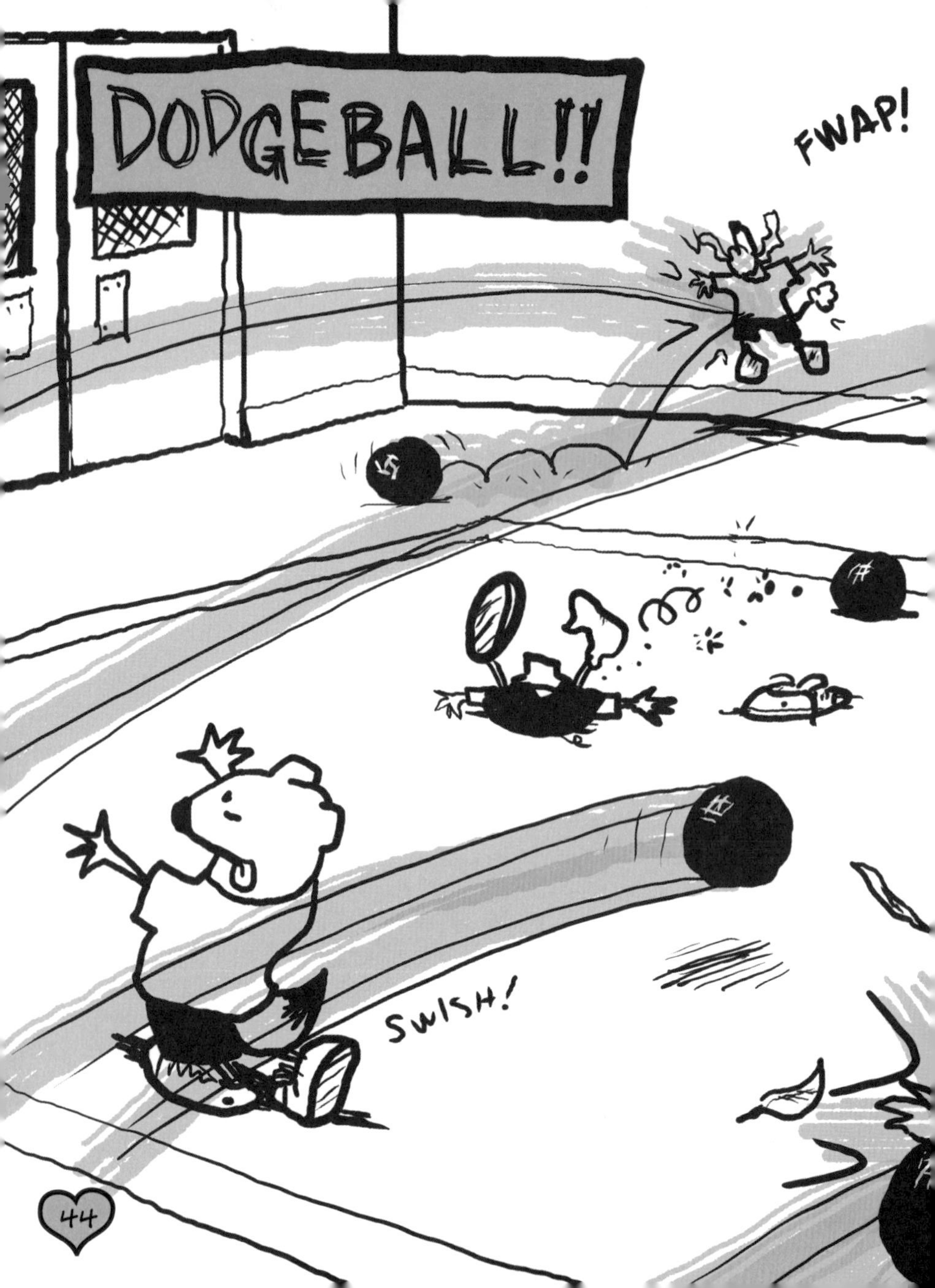
DODGEBALL!!
FWAP!
SWISH!

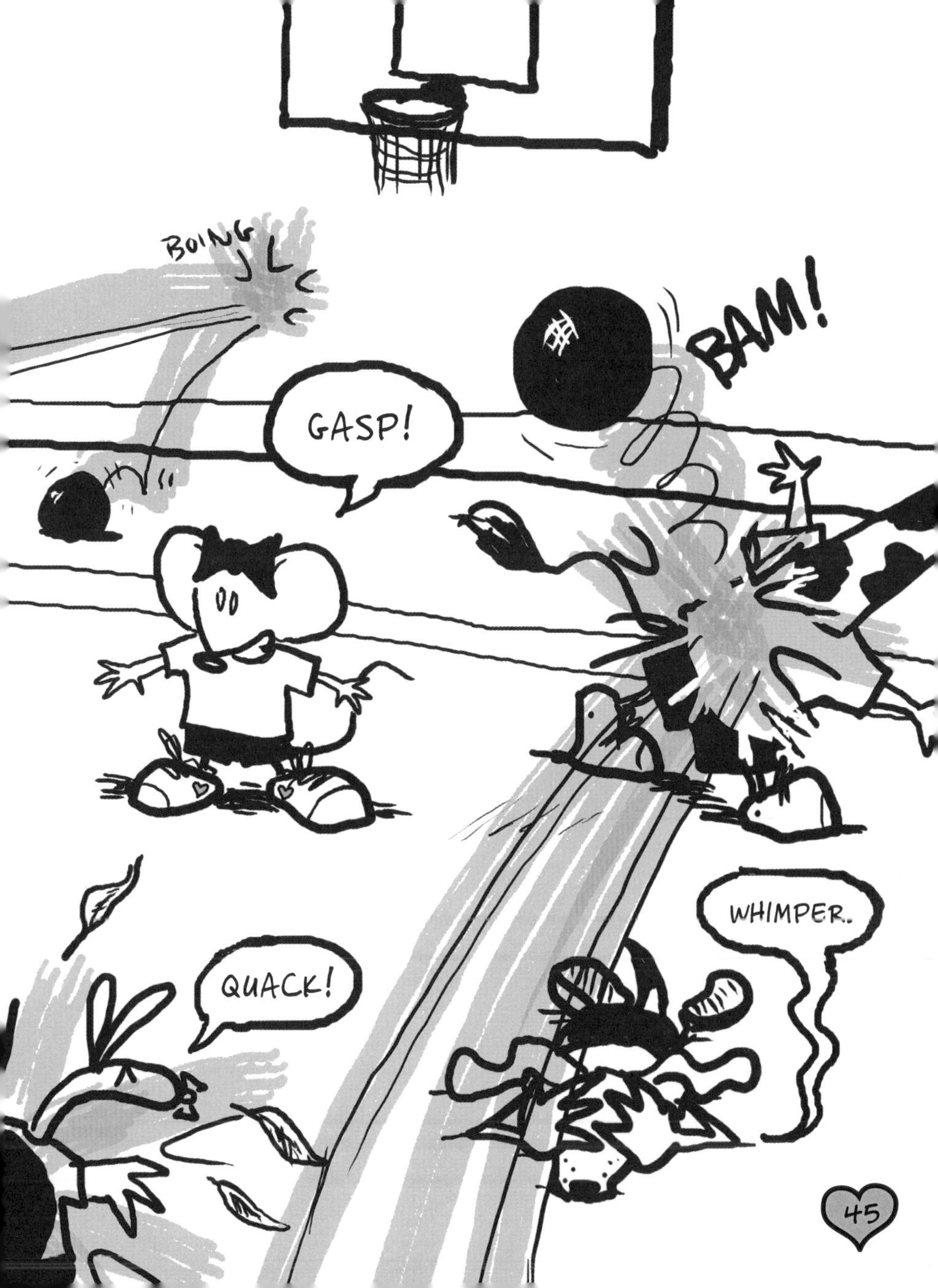
BOING
BAM!
GASP!
WHIMPER..
QUACK!

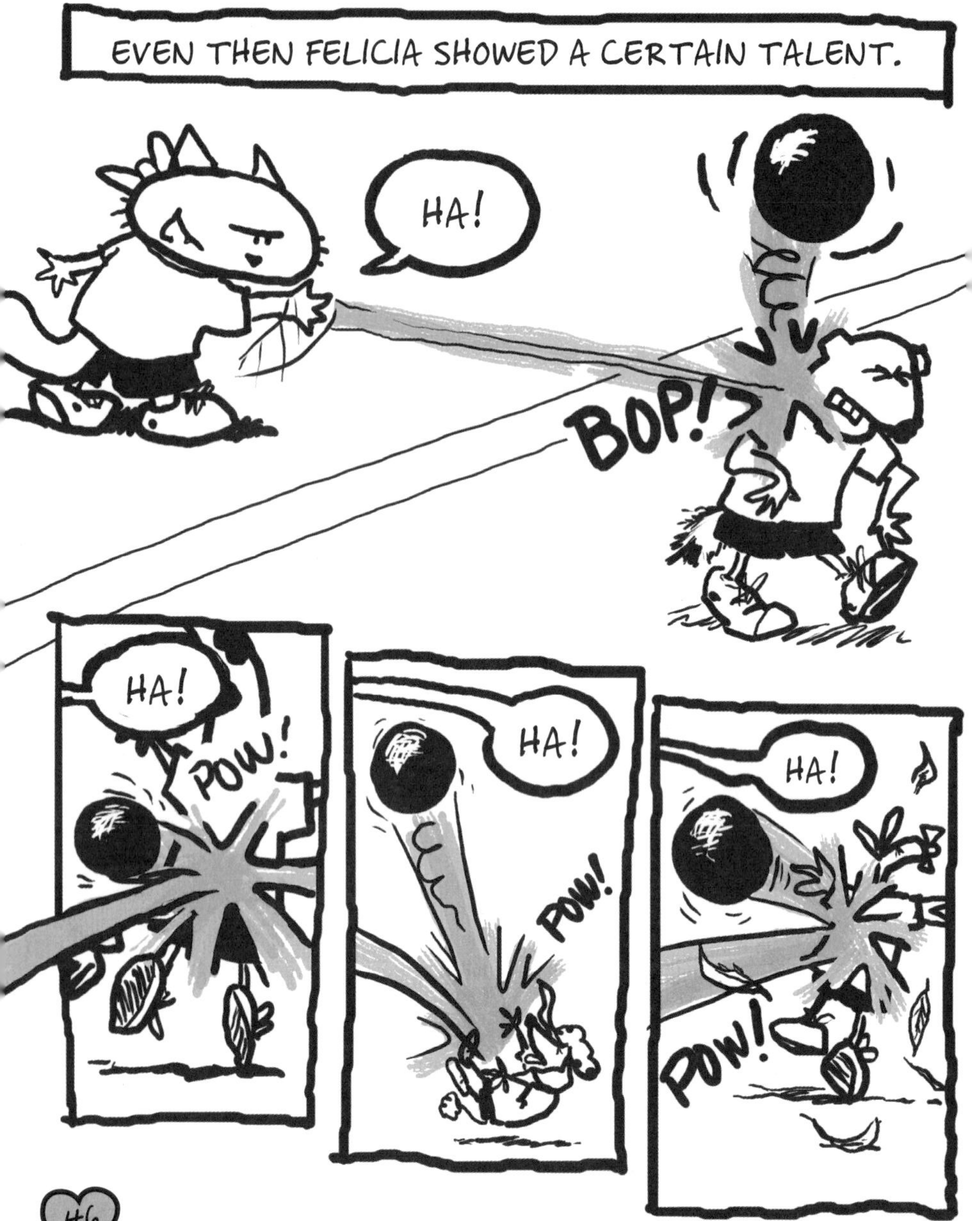
EVEN THEN FELICIA SHOWED A CERTAIN TALENT.
HA!
BOP!
HA!
POW!
HA!
POW!
HA!
POW!

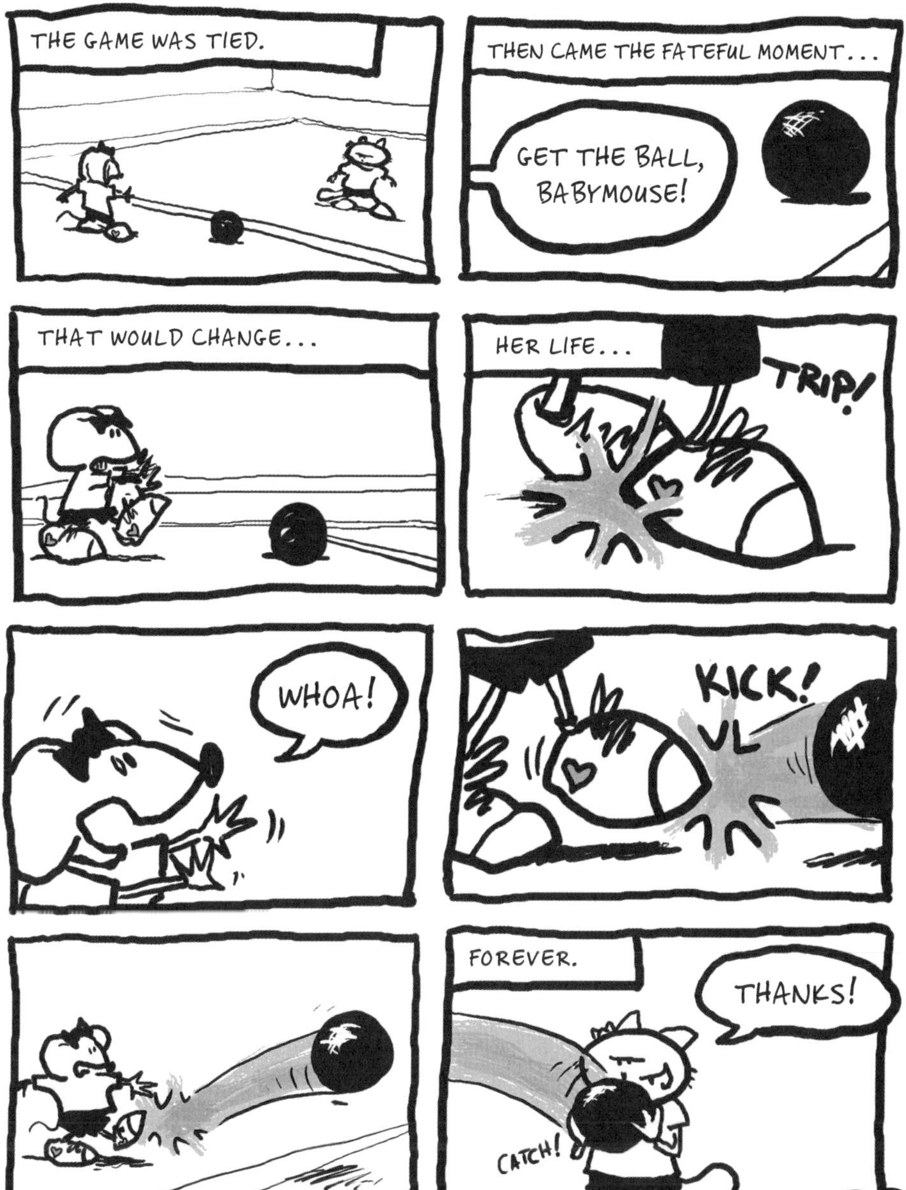
THE GAME WAS TIED.
THEN CAME THE FATEFUL MOMENT . . .
GET THE BALL, BABYMOUSE!
THAT WOULD CHANGE . . .
HER LIFE . . .
TRIP!
WHOA!
KICK!
FOREVER.
THANKS!
CATCH!

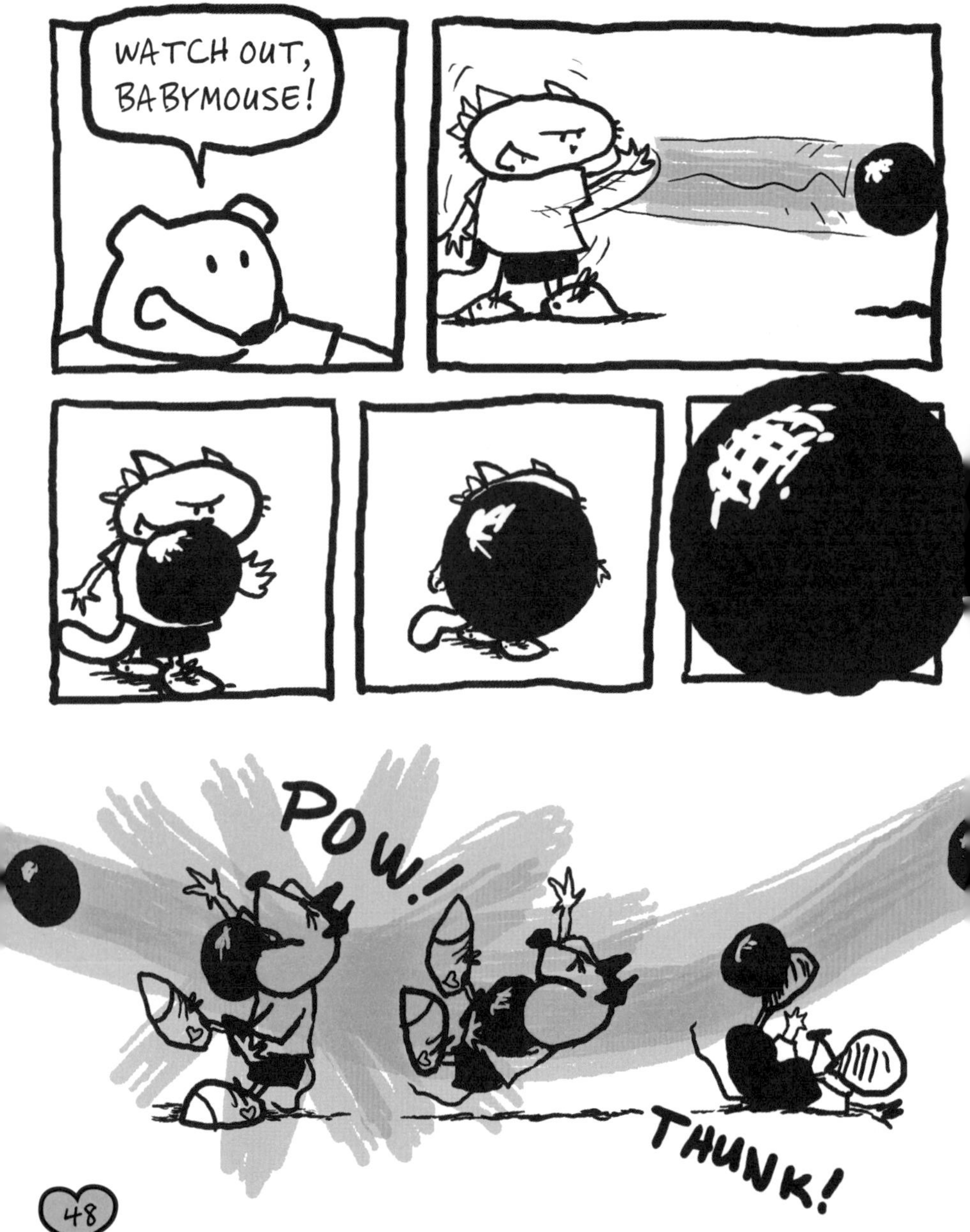
WATCH OUT, BABYMOUSE!
POW!
THUNK!

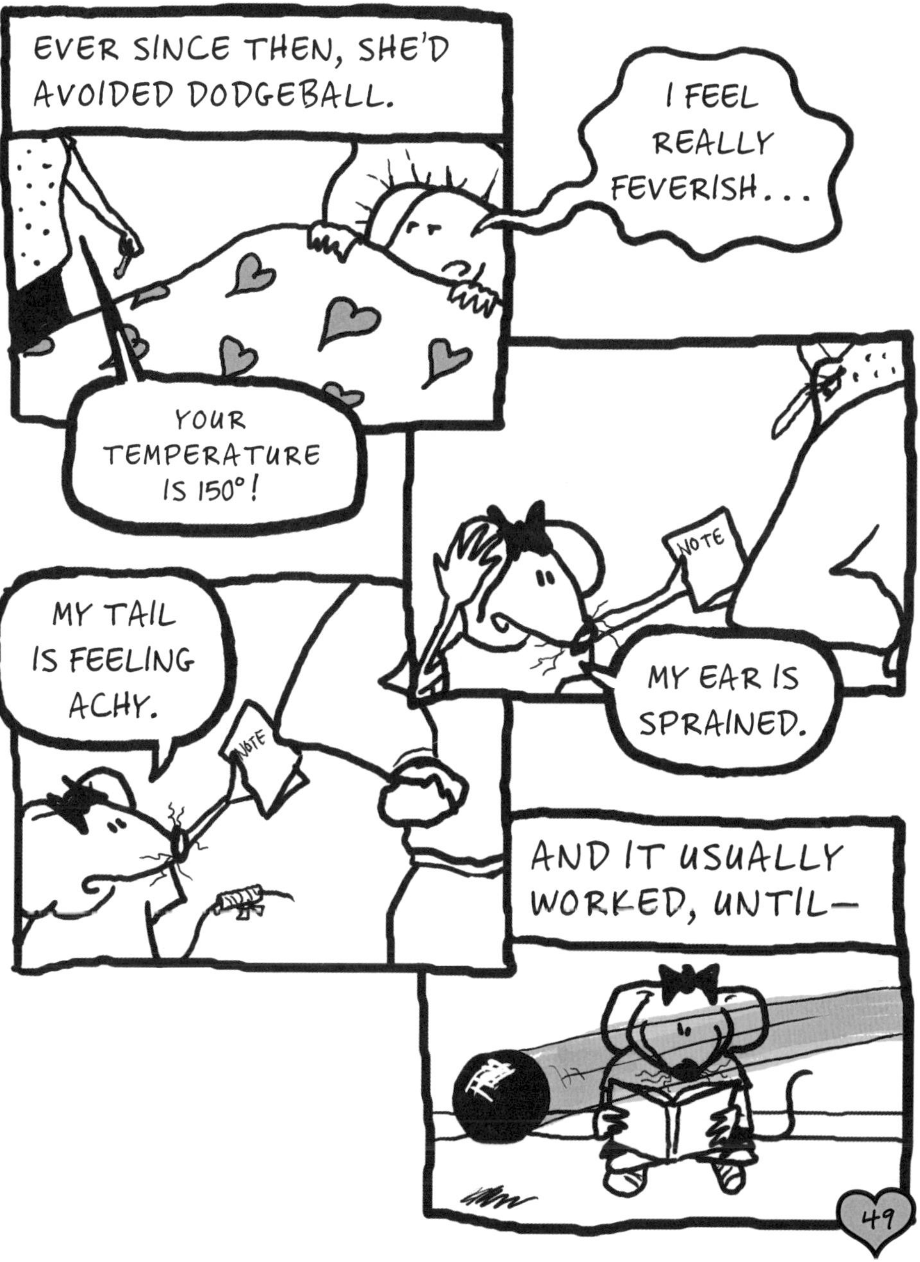
EVER SINCE THEN, SHE'D AVOIDED DODGEBALL.
I FEEL REALLY FEVERISH...
YOUR TEMPERATURE IS 150°!
NOTE
MY EAR IS SPRAINED.
MY TAIL IS FEELING ACHY.
NOTE
AND IT USUALLY WORKED, UNTIL—

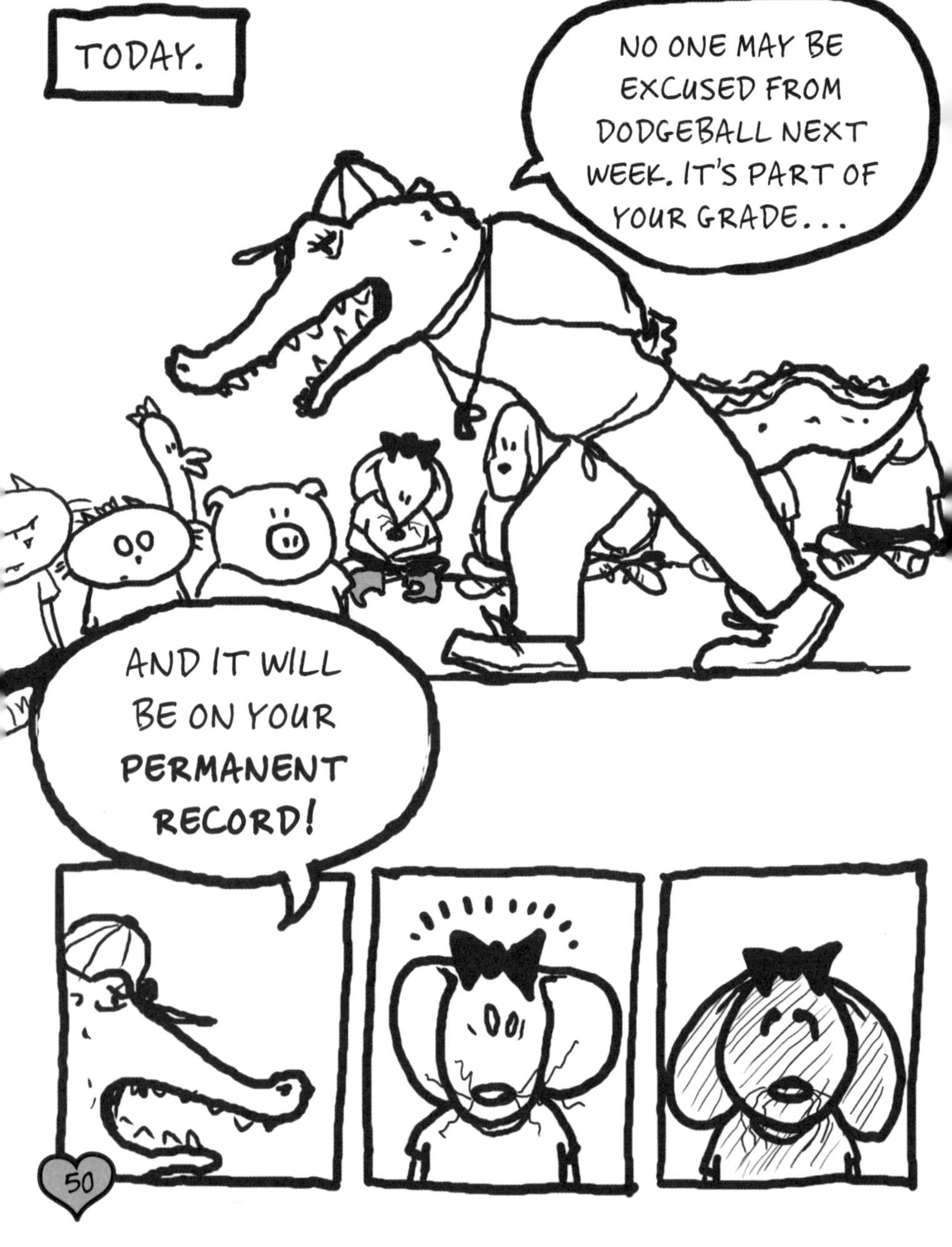
TODAY.
NO ONE MAY BE EXCUSED FROM DODGEBALL NEXT WEEK. IT'S PART OF YOUR GRADE...
AND IT WILL BE ON YOUR PERMANENT RECORD!

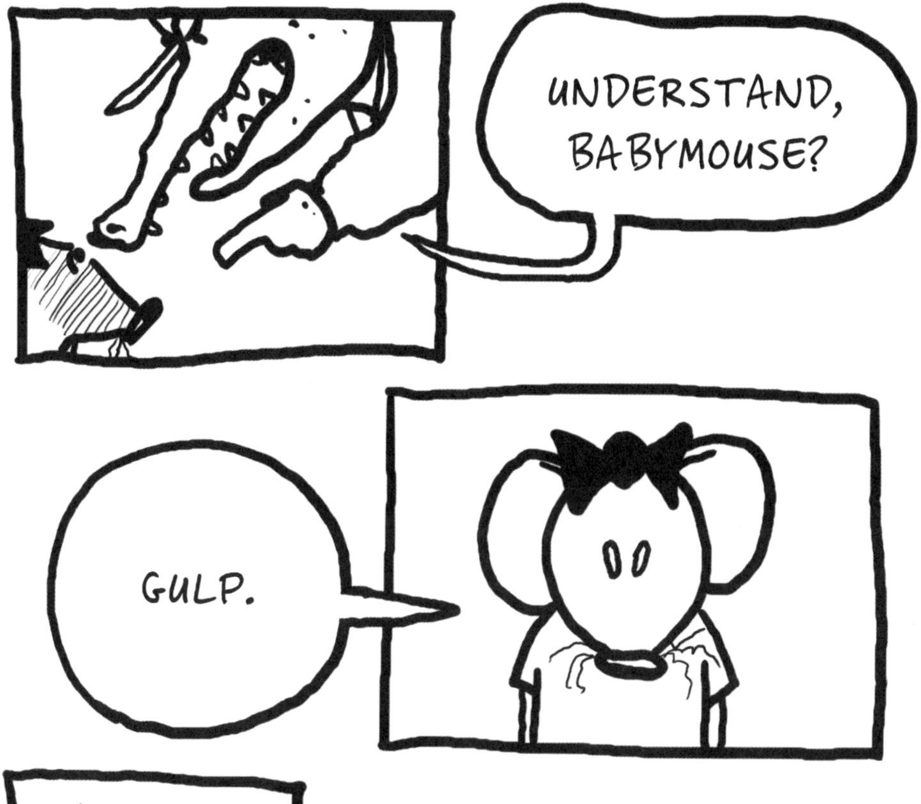
UNDERSTAND, BABYMOUSE?
GULP.
LATER...
WHAT AM I GOING TO DO?
MAYBE YOU JUST NEED TO PRACTICE.

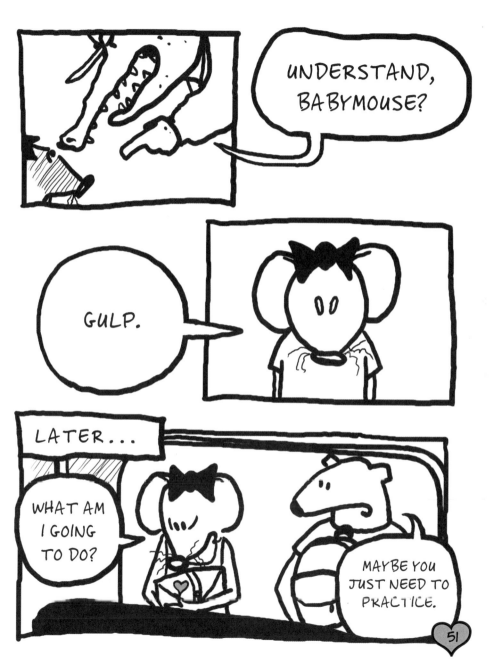

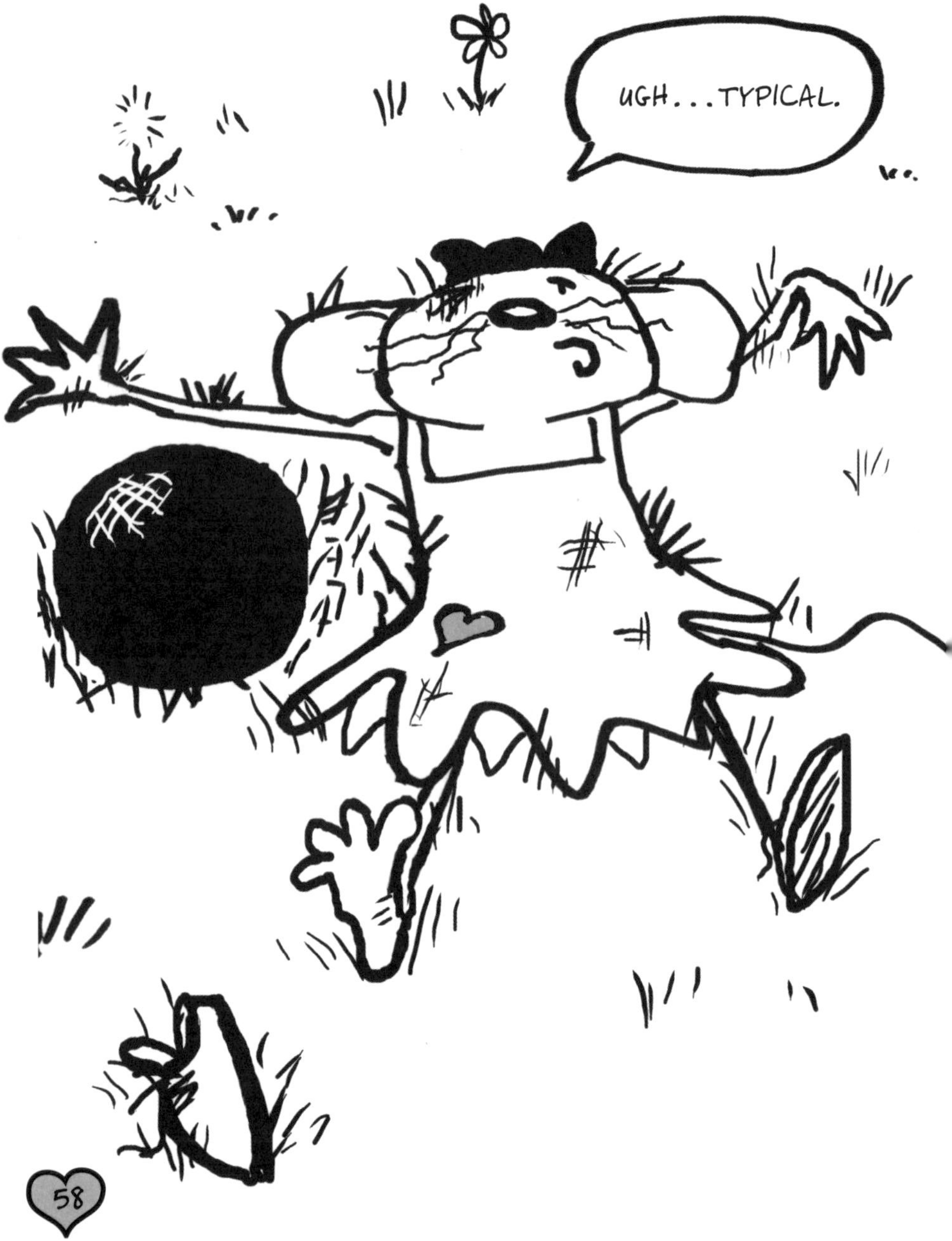
UGH...TYPICAL.

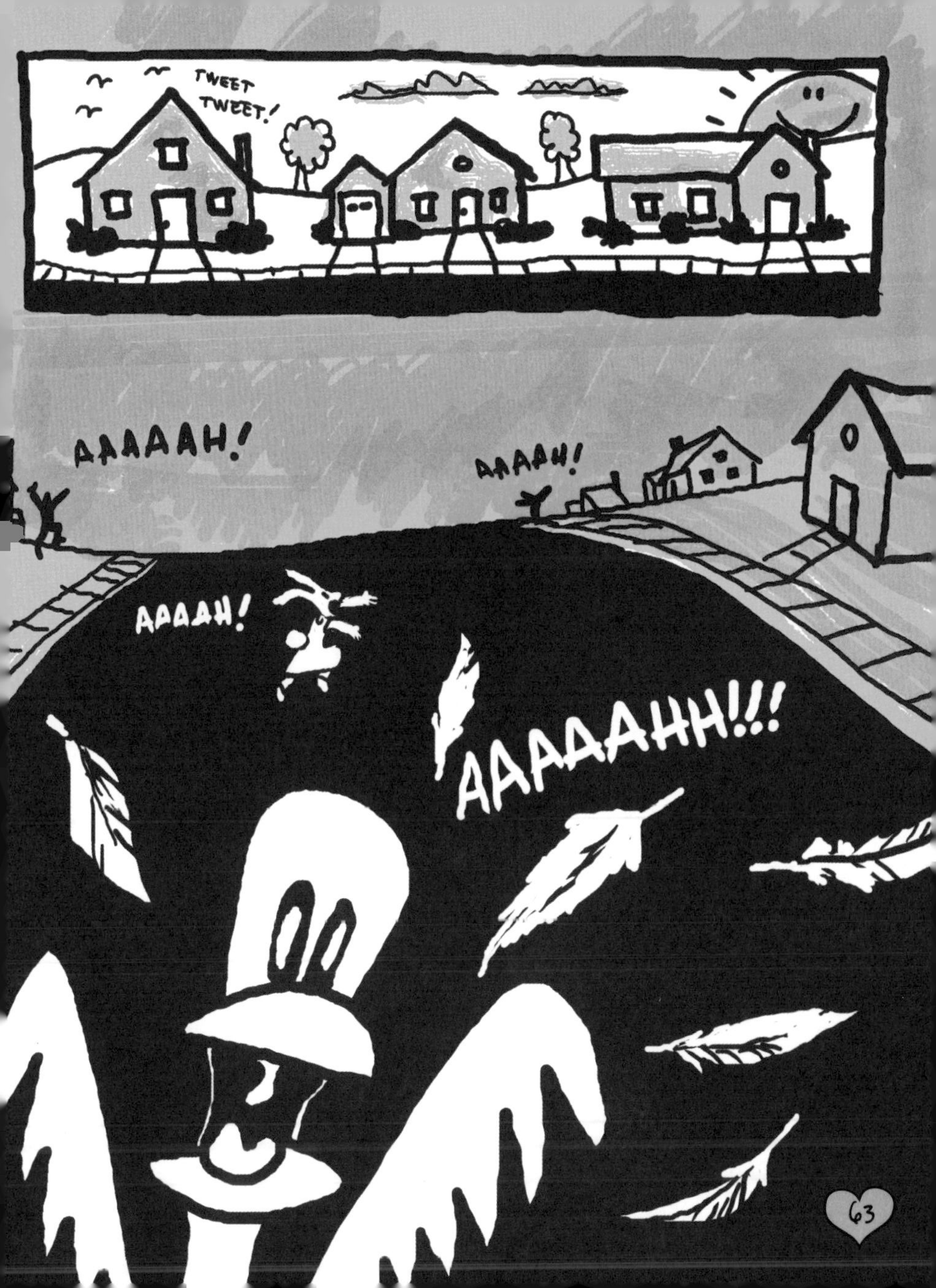
TWEET TWEET!
AAAAAH!
AAAAH!
AAAAH!
AAAAAHH!!!

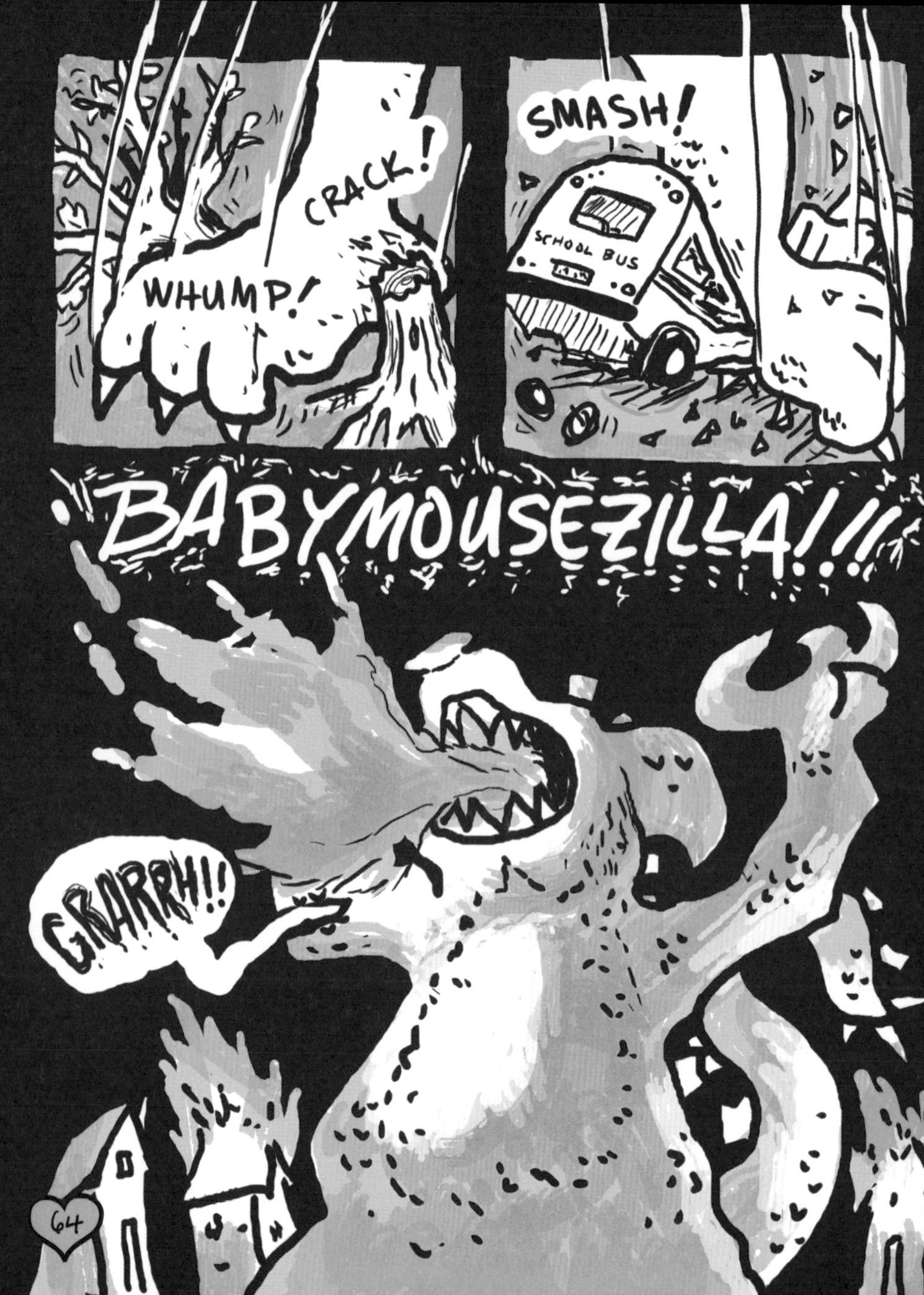
CRACK!
WHUMP!
SMASH!
SCHOOL BUS
BABYMOUSEZILLA!!!
GRARRH!!

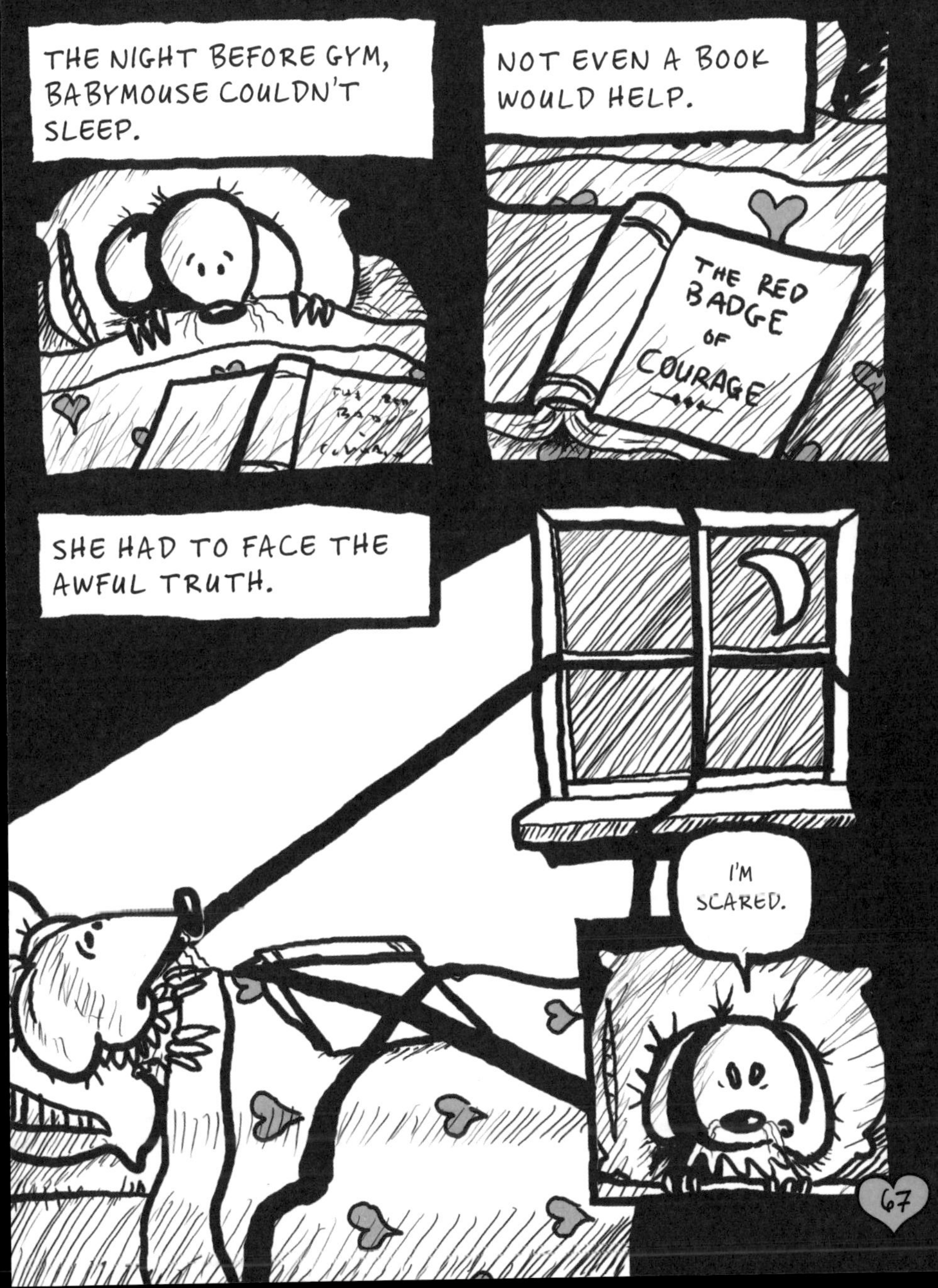
THE NIGHT BEFORE GYM, BABYMOUSE COULDN'T SLEEP.
NOT EVEN A BOOK WOULD HELP.
THE RED BADGE OF COURAGE
SHE HAD TO FACE THE AWFUL TRUTH.
I'M SCARED.

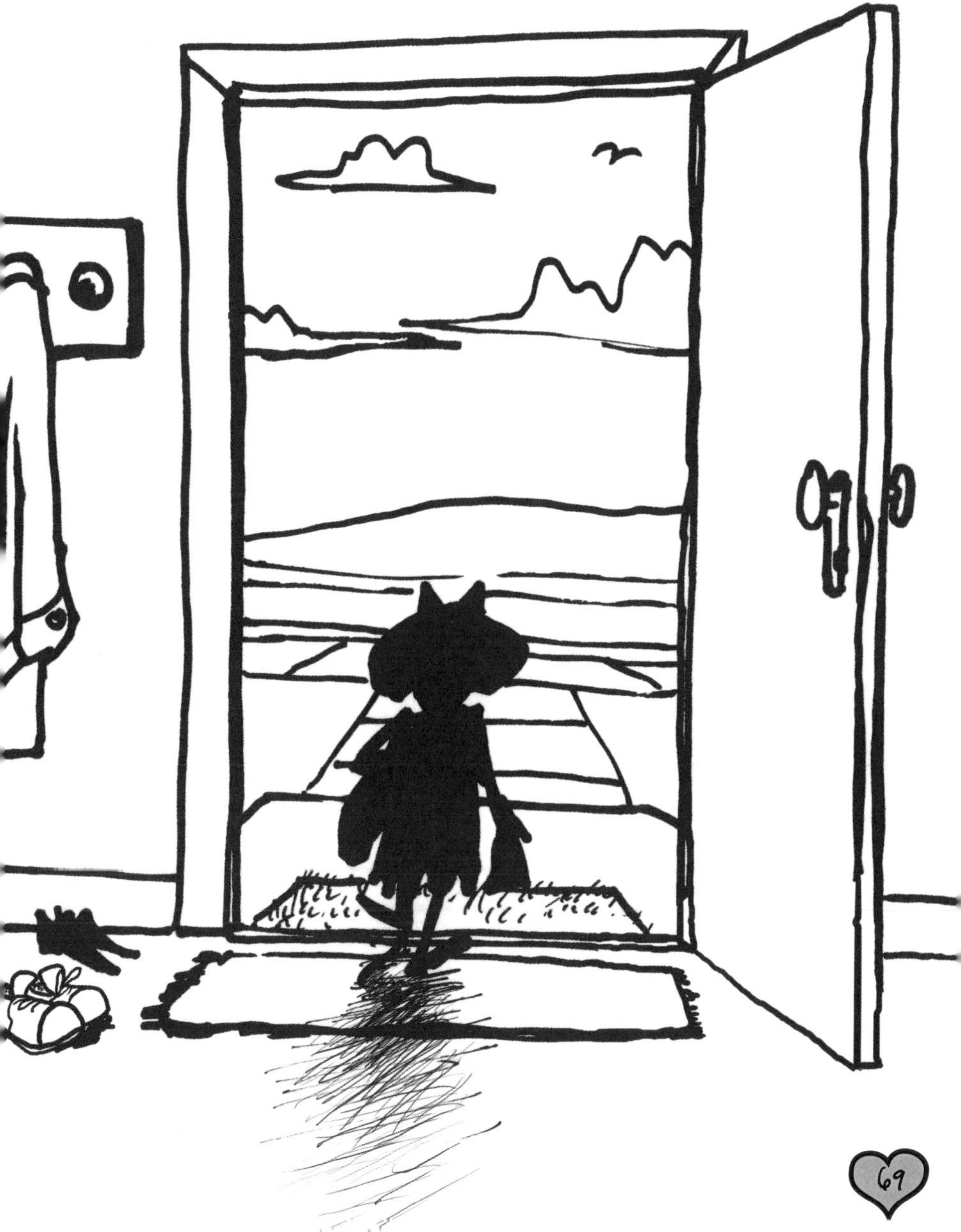

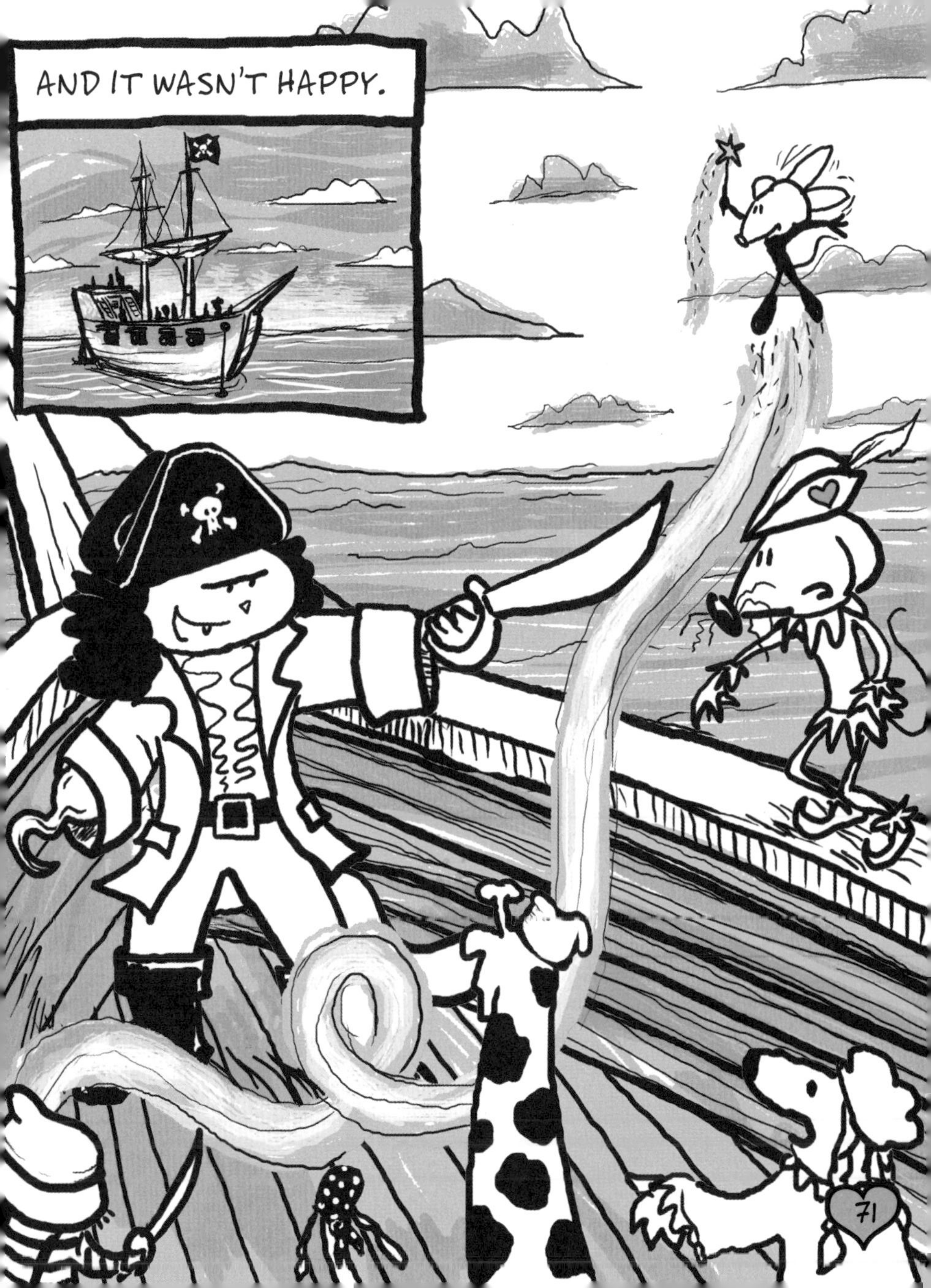
AND IT WASN'T HAPPY.

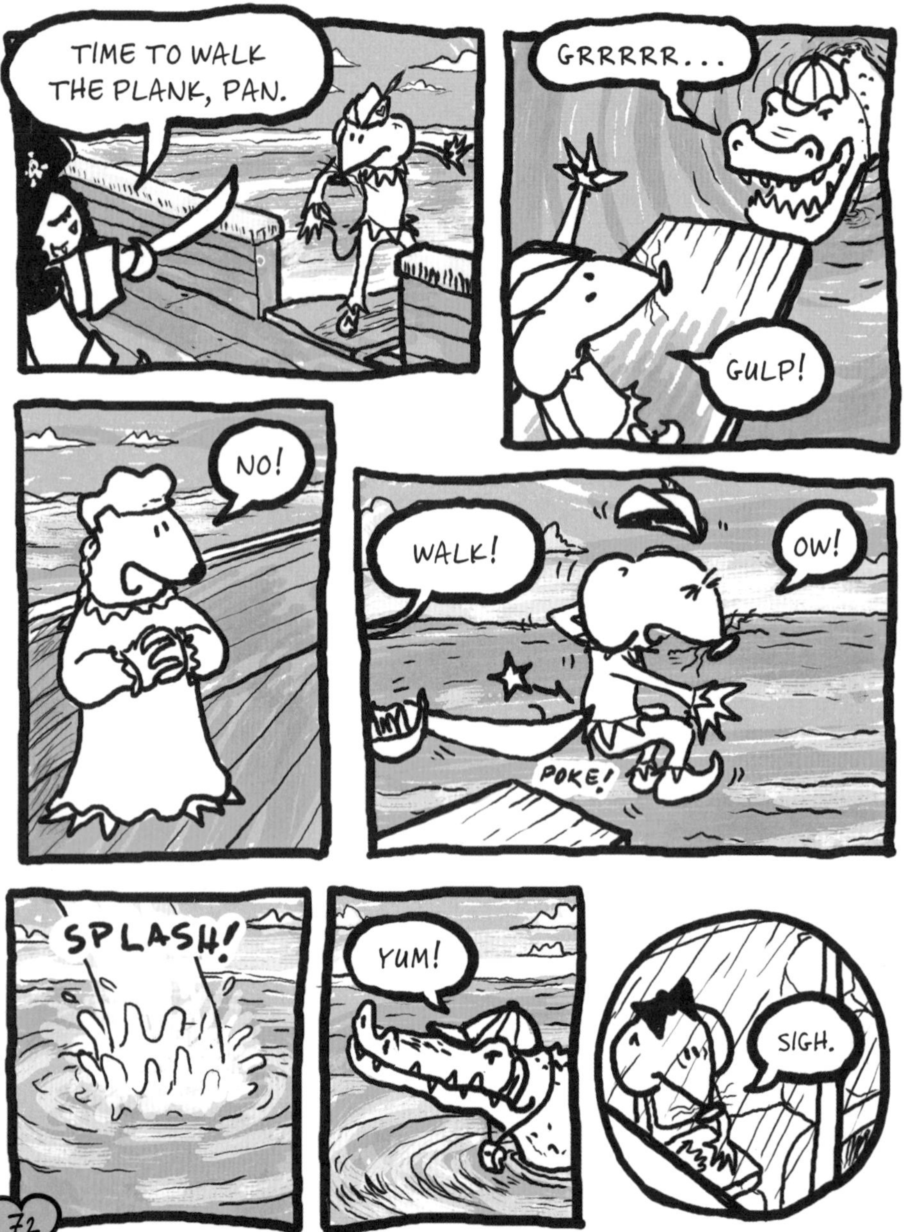
TIME TO WALK THE PLANK, PAN.
GRRRRR...
GULP!
NO!
WALK!
OW!
POKE!
SPLASH!
YUM!
SIGH.

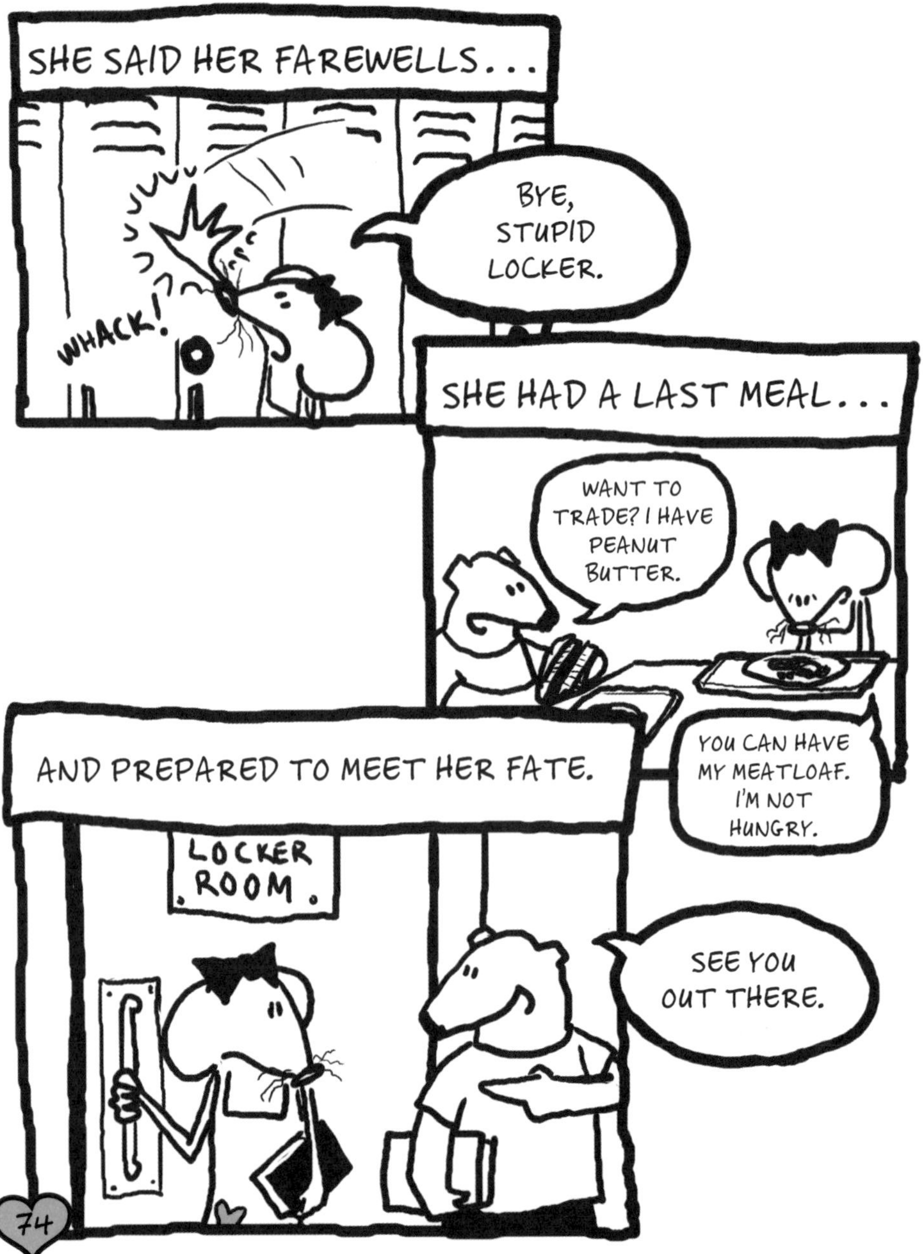
SHE SAID HER FAREWELLS...
WHACK!
BYE, STUPID LOCKER.
SHE HAD A LAST MEAL...
WANT TO TRADE? I HAVE PEANUT BUTTER.
YOU CAN HAVE MY MEATLOAF. I'M NOT HUNGRY.
AND PREPARED TO MEET HER FATE.
LOCKER ROOM
SEE YOU OUT THERE.

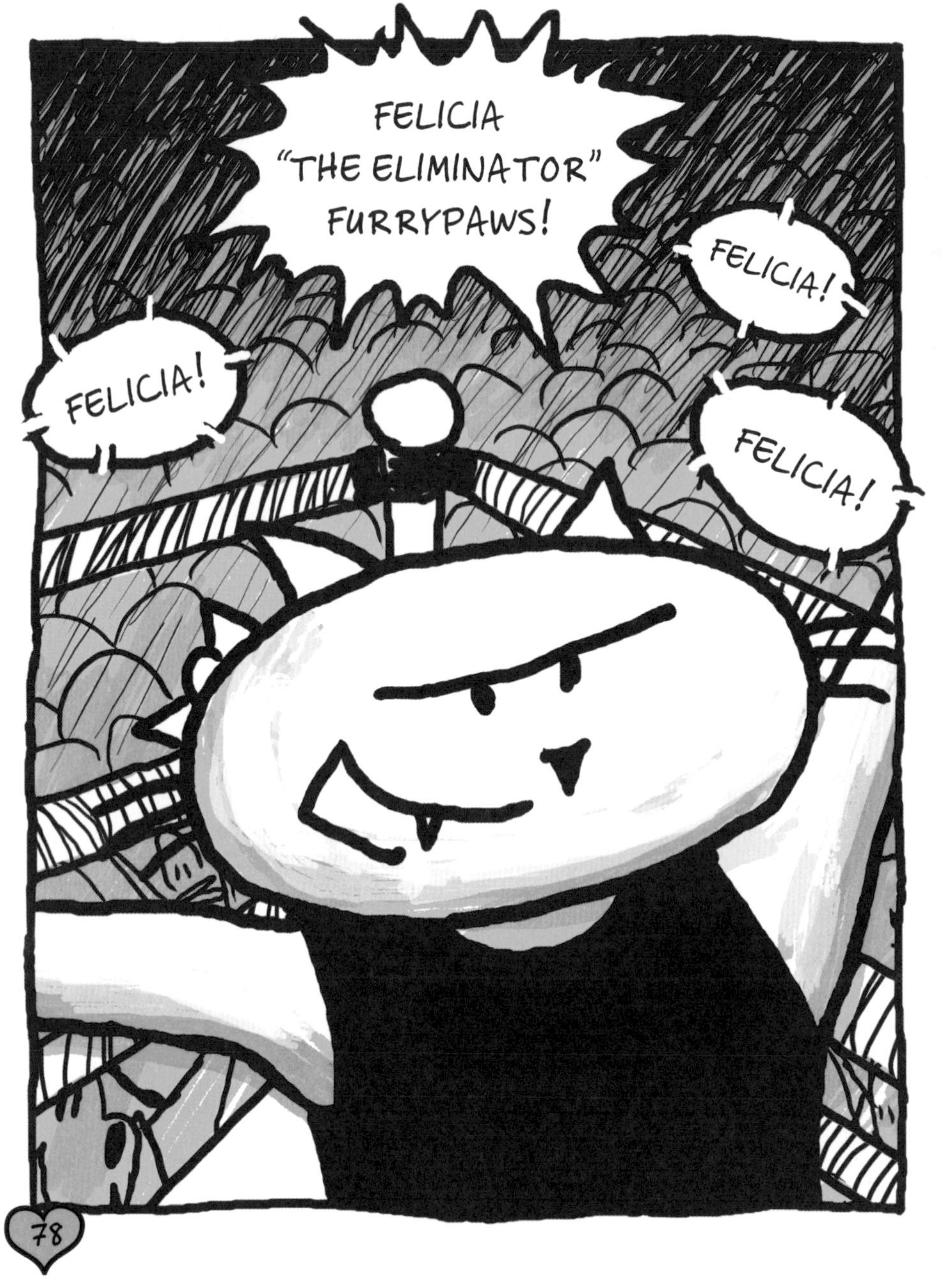
FELICIA
"THE ELIMINATOR"
FURRYPAWS!
FELICIA!
FELICIA!
FELICIA!

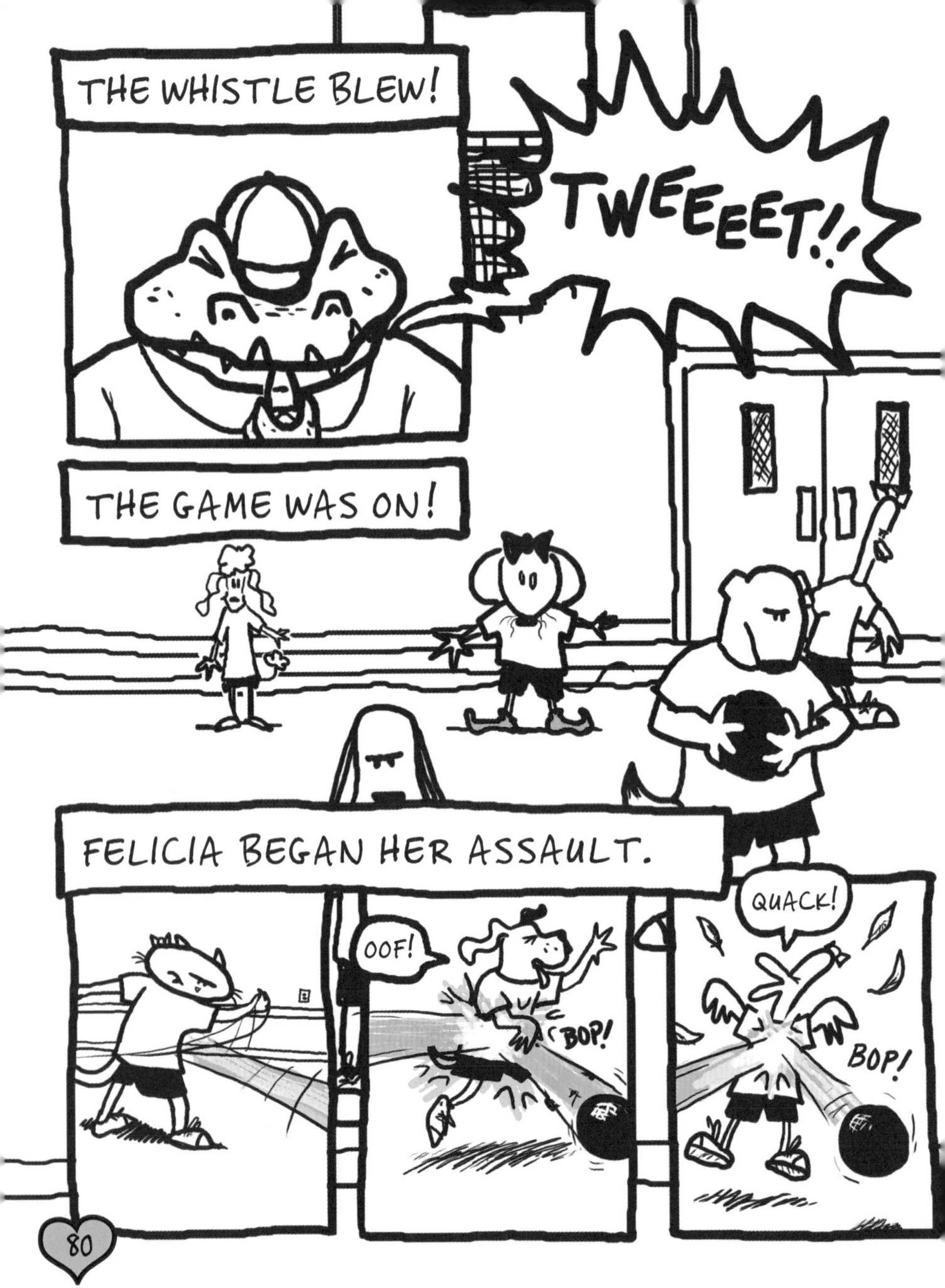
THE WHISTLE BLEW!
TWEEEEET!!!
THE GAME WAS ON!
FELICIA BEGAN HER ASSAULT.
OOF!
BOP!
QUACK!
BOP!

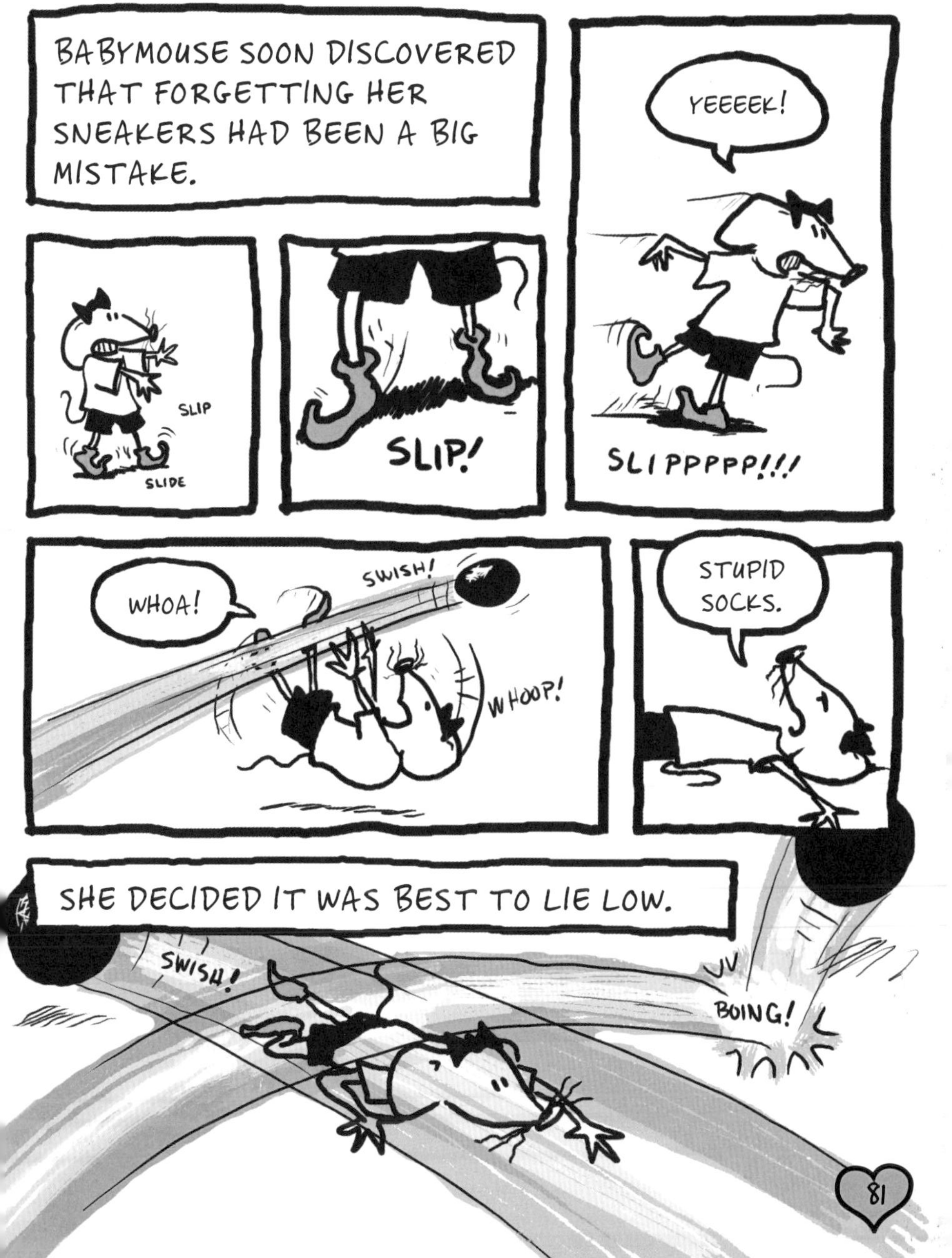
BABYMOUSE SOON DISCOVERED THAT FORGETTING HER SNEAKERS HAD BEEN A BIG MISTAKE.
SLIP
SLIDE
SLIP!
YEEEEK!
SLIPPPPP!!!
WHOA!
SWISH!
WHOOP!
STUPID SOCKS.
SHE DECIDED IT WAS BEST TO LIE LOW.
SWISH!
BOING!

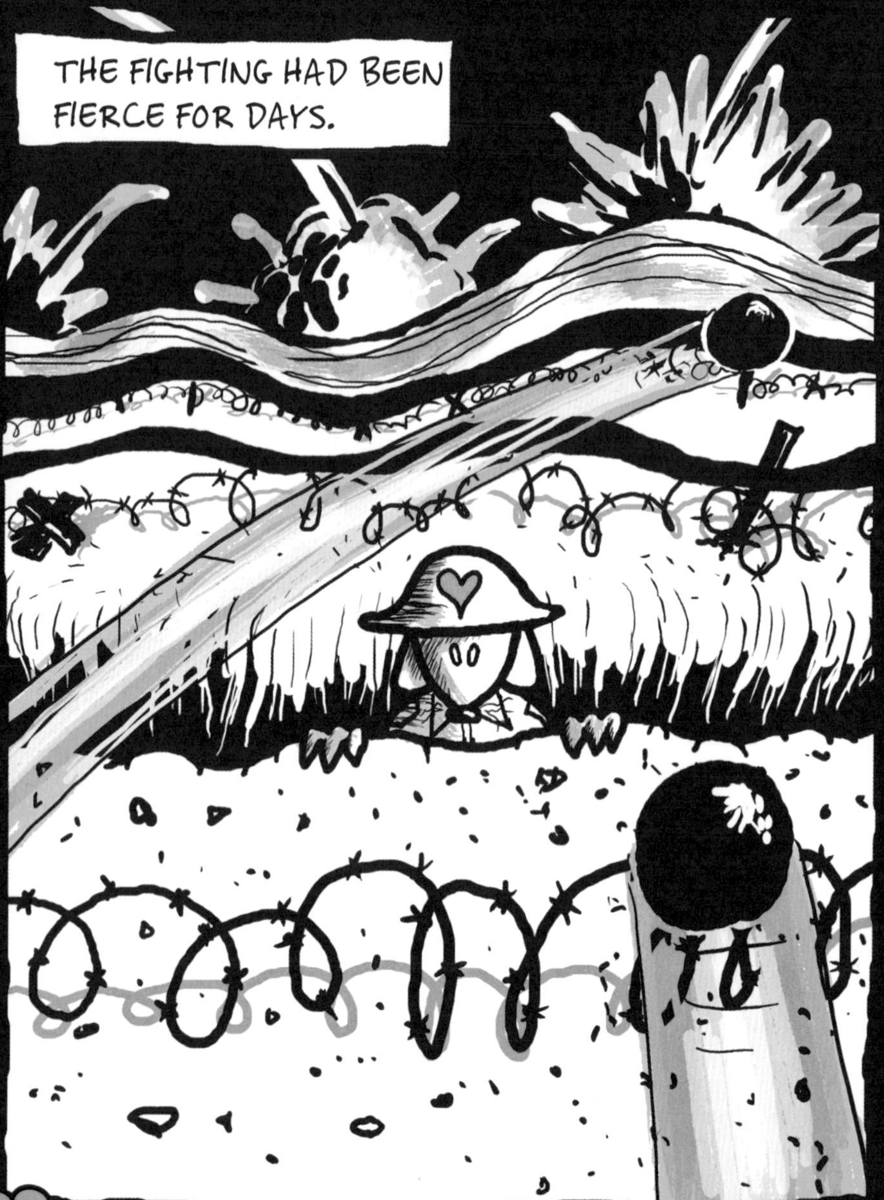
THE FIGHTING HAD BEEN FIERCE FOR DAYS.

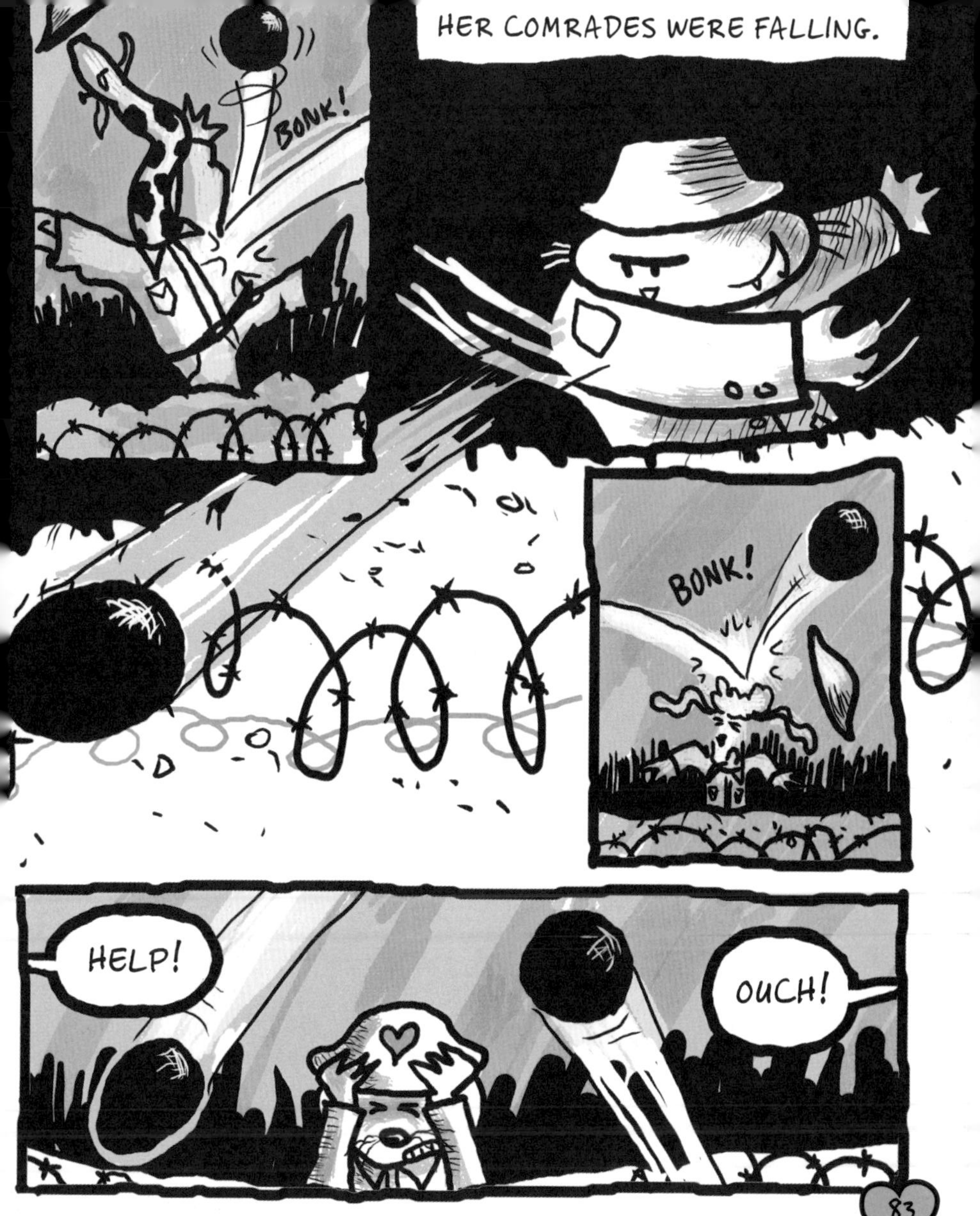
HER COMRADES WERE FALLING.
BONK!
BONK!
HELP!
OUCH!

84

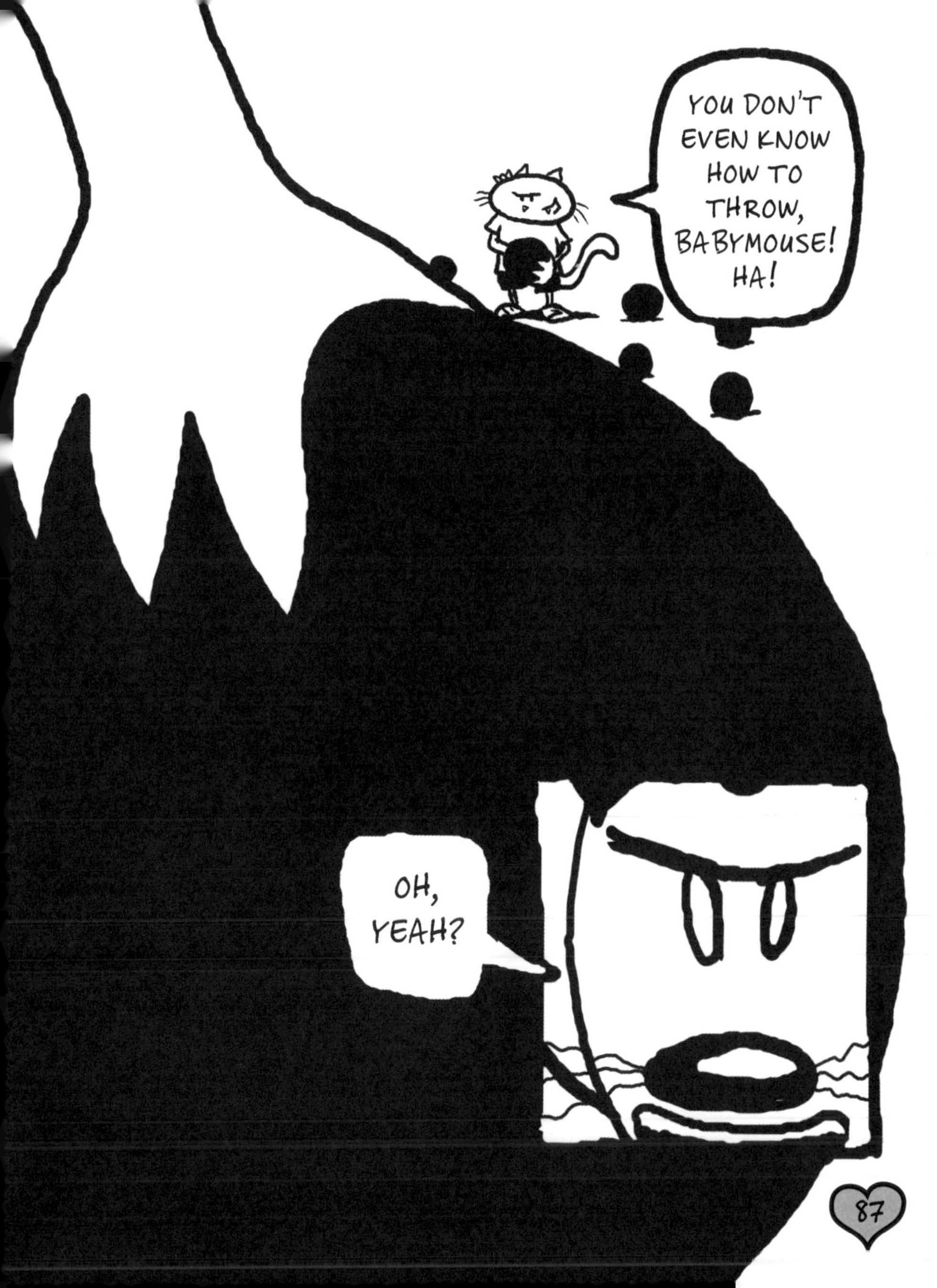
YOU DON'T EVEN KNOW HOW TO THROW, BABYMOUSE! HA!
OH, YEAH?

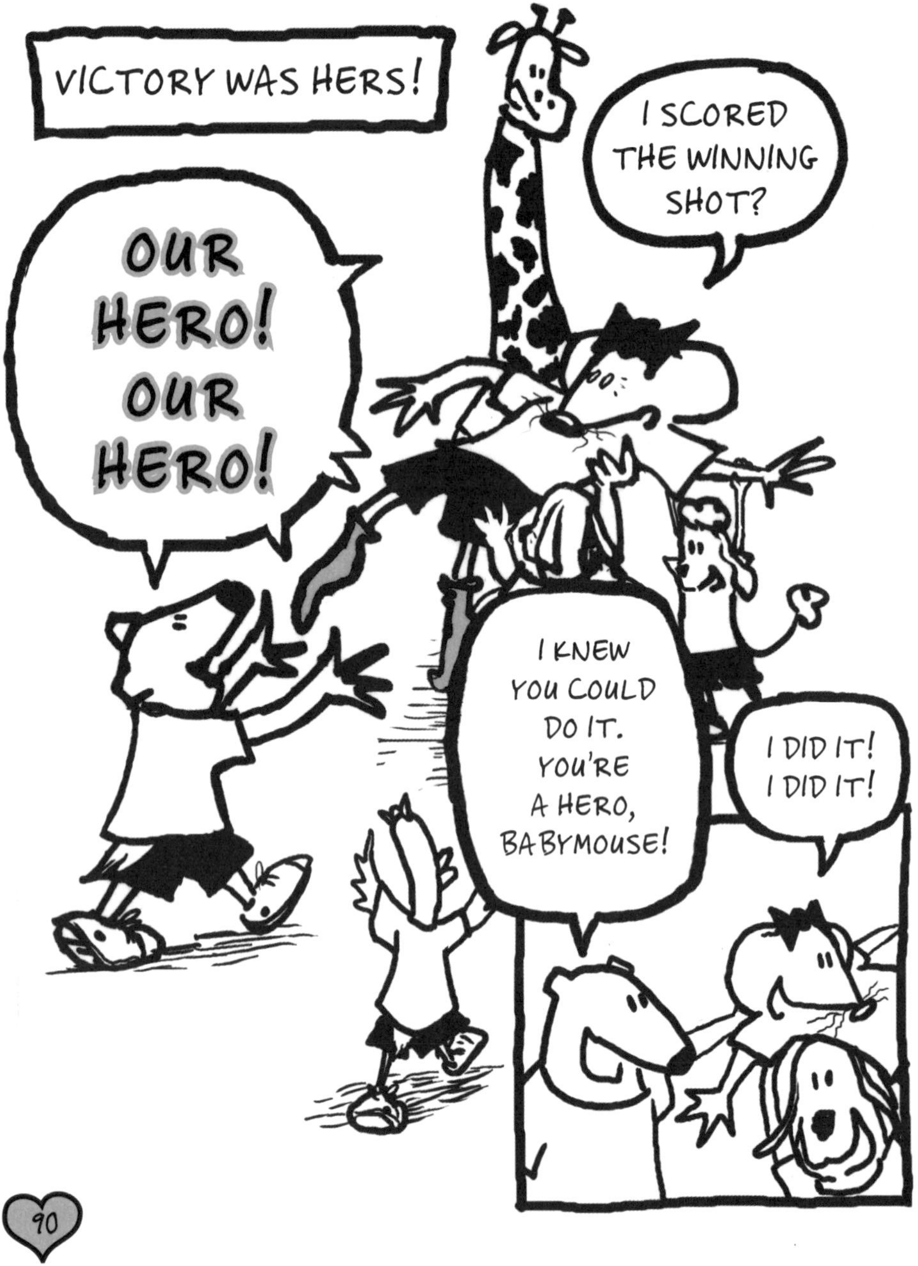
VICTORY WAS HERS!
I SCORED THE WINNING SHOT?
OUR HERO! OUR HERO!
I KNEW YOU COULD DO IT. YOU'RE A HERO, BABYMOUSE!
I DID IT! I DID IT!

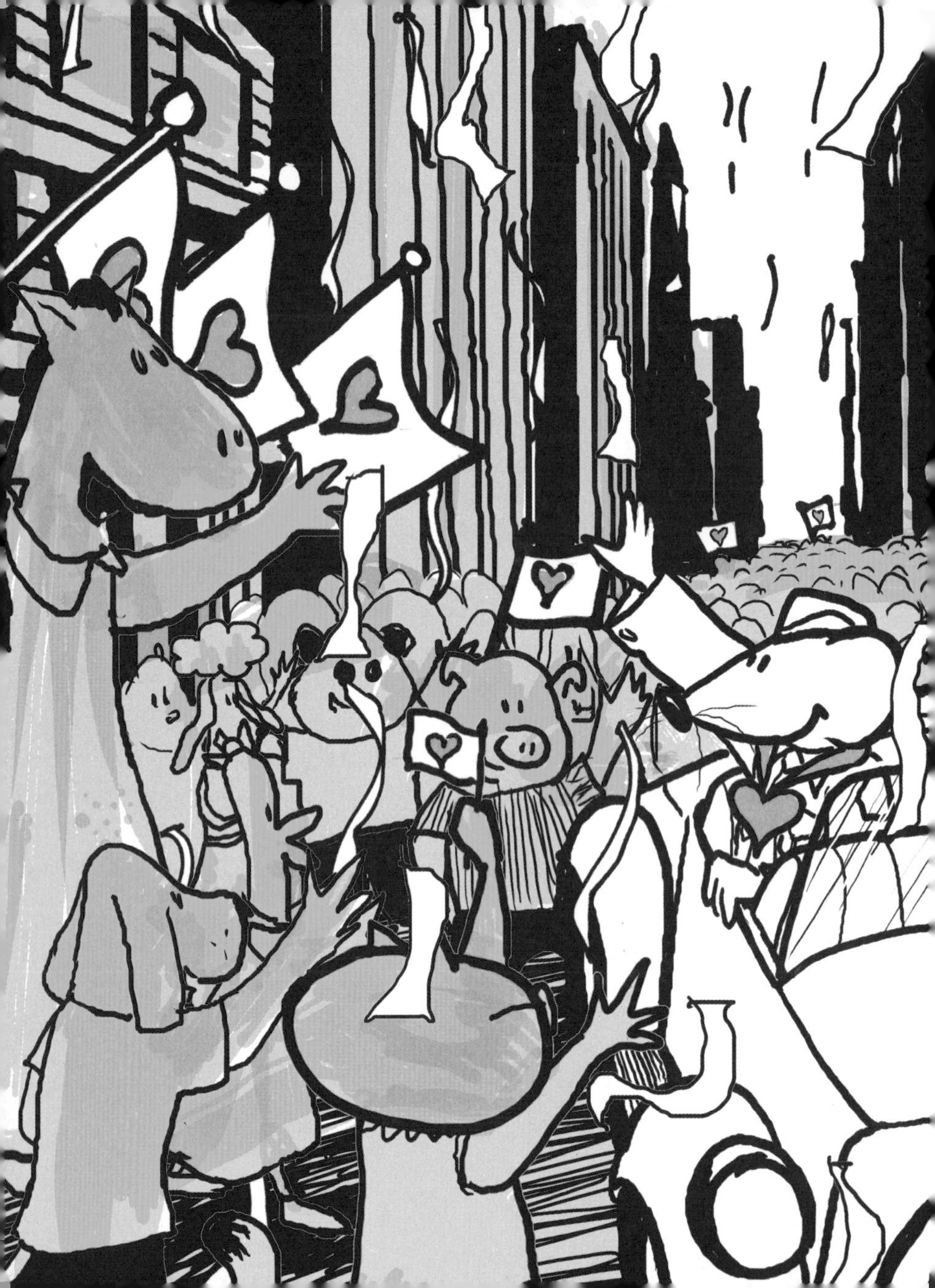

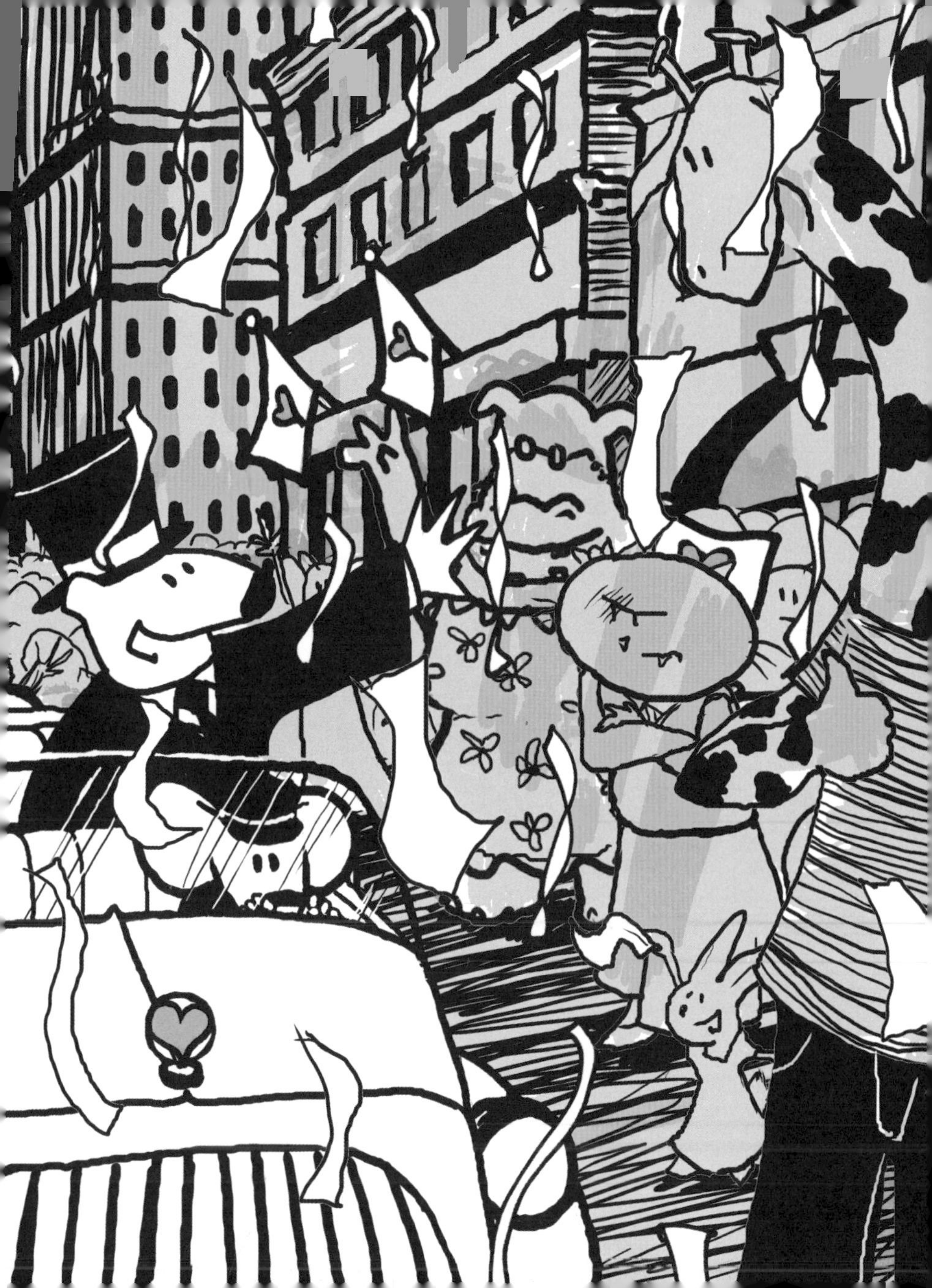